Forever Friends: Heartbreaking and Touching Dog Stories

Morgan B. Blake

Published by CopyPeople.com, 2024.

Table of Contents

Get A Free Book At: https://free.copypeople.com

1. https://copypeople.com/

2. https://copypeople.com/

3. https://free.copypeople.com

Whispers in the Wind

Max had always been the first to greet Henry when he returned home, his tail wagging in time with the rhythmic sound of boots hitting the porch. For years, the old German Shepherd had waited for Henry's footsteps, the bond between them as inseparable as air and breath. They had faced war, hardship, and loss together, both battered but unbroken, both finding solace in each other's presence. But now, Henry was gone.

It had been nearly a year since the war veteran's passing, and Max, with his silver muzzle and clouded eyes, had not moved from his post by the front door. He still believed, as he had all his life, that his master would return one day. The house that once rang with laughter, the clink of mugs, and the soft hum of the radio now sat silent, its windows darkened. The family that Henry had left behind had moved away, leaving only Max to guard the fading memory of a life long past.

Max hadn't always been a solitary creature. There had been a time when children ran through the house, filling it with noise and joy. But now, the garden was overgrown, the swing in the yard rusted, and the air around the house felt thick with the weight of forgotten moments. Every day, Max lay on the porch, staring out at the empty road, his ears perked for the sound of Henry's truck pulling into the driveway.

The days grew longer, the shadows of dusk creeping across the porch as the world moved on. Sometimes, Max would hear the distant laughter of other dogs, playing in their yards or chasing after their masters, but all of that seemed a world away. His eyes would narrow as if willing the world to stop, to freeze, so that the moment could last just a little longer.

It wasn't that he didn't know the truth. He had felt the absence of Henry long before the family left. He had seen the tears in the old man's eyes as he said goodbye, as if even he knew the end was near. But

Max couldn't understand it, couldn't grasp that the steady hand that had always cared for him, that had fed him, patted him, and whispered promises of never leaving, was now gone forever.

One chilly autumn morning, a figure appeared at the edge of the driveway. Max's heart skipped a beat. His tail thumped softly against the porch, but it wasn't Henry. The man who approached was dressed in dark clothes, his face shadowed by a cap. The stranger moved slowly toward the house, his steps tentative, almost as if he were unsure whether he belonged there.

Max didn't bark, didn't wag his tail in excitement. Instead, he watched, his old eyes narrowing. The stranger reached the porch and stopped in front of Max, his hand shaking slightly as he knelt down. "It's been a long time, old boy," he said quietly. "I'm sorry. I never got to say goodbye."

Max sniffed the man's hand, his tail betraying him with a slow, hesitant wag. The man stroked his head, his hand trembling as he did so. "I was his brother," he continued, his voice thick with emotion. "I should have been here sooner."

Max blinked, his head tilting to the side as he absorbed the words, unsure of their meaning. The man stood, a heavy sigh escaping him. "I came to bring you something," he said, turning to the car parked by the road. He returned moments later, holding something wrapped in cloth.

Max watched as the man unwrapped the bundle, revealing a small, worn leather collar—Henry's collar. The man placed it gently around Max's neck, his fingers brushing against the dog's fur one last time. "He loved you, Max. He always loved you," the man whispered, before turning to leave.

Max stood there, his eyes following the man's retreating figure, his heart heavy with the weight of understanding. The collar felt familiar, but it wasn't the same. The wind stirred the leaves around him, as if the world itself was whispering something he couldn't quite hear.

For the first time in months, Max didn't wait for footsteps. He didn't search the horizon for a truck. Instead, he lay down on the porch, his eyes half-closed, the collar resting lightly on his neck. The wind, as always, would carry whispers of the past.

And for Max, that would be enough.

The Last Sunset

Bella's fur had once been a glossy golden hue, but now it was dulled with age and illness. She had lived a tough life before coming to the foster home—abandoned in a dirty alley, starving, and sick. Her ribs showed beneath the sparse coat, and her eyes were haunted, as though she had witnessed too much for a dog her size. Yet, in the quiet warmth of her new home, she began to change.

Her foster parents, Emma and Alex, had taken her in without hesitation when the shelter had called. Bella had been diagnosed with a terminal illness—cancer that had spread too far for any kind of treatment. The vet gave her only a few months to live, and Emma and Alex knew that they couldn't give Bella a cure, but they could offer her something far more valuable: love.

In the first few days, Bella hid in the corners of the house, her head low, her tail tucked between her legs. She didn't trust anyone, and who could blame her? The world had shown her nothing but cruelty. But Emma and Alex didn't give up. They gave Bella space, never forcing her to interact but always offering her comfort—soft words, gentle touches, and warm meals. Slowly, Bella's mistrust started to fade, replaced by cautious curiosity.

By the time the first month had passed, Bella began to follow Emma around the house, her tail wagging in the smallest of motions. She would lie at Alex's feet while he worked in his office, her eyes soft and trusting. They knew the time they had with her was limited, but each day they watched her become more herself—more relaxed, more present. And for Bella, it was the first time in her life she had truly felt at home.

Bella had one particular spot in the house where she loved to sit—the front porch. It was a small area, just big enough for a chair and a table, but from there, she could watch the world go by. The sun would dip below the horizon every evening, painting the sky in shades of orange and pink, and Bella would sit, her eyes half-closed, enjoying the warmth of the setting sun.

It became their routine. Emma and Alex would join her on the porch, their quiet conversations blending with the sounds of birdsong and the distant hum of traffic. Bella would rest her head on Emma's lap, and Alex would scratch behind her ears, both of them lost in the simplicity of the moment.

But as the days passed, Bella's illness began to take its toll. Her once-vibrant energy waned. She could no longer walk as far or play with the same enthusiasm. Emma and Alex watched helplessly as the sparkle in Bella's eyes slowly dimmed. They could feel the weight of her suffering, the inevitability of the end creeping closer with each passing day. But they never spoke of it. They didn't need to. The love between them was enough to fill the silence.

One evening, as the sun began to set, Bella took her usual place on the porch, her body trembling slightly with exhaustion. Emma and Alex sat beside her, the three of them still and quiet, watching as the last rays of daylight disappeared over the horizon. Bella's breathing was shallow, and her once bright eyes seemed distant.

As the night air grew cooler, Emma gently lifted Bella's head into her lap, feeling the softness of her fur, the stillness that had overtaken her body. Bella looked up at her, a final flicker of recognition in her gaze before she closed her eyes. For a moment, time seemed to stretch, the quiet beauty of the sunset mingling with the sadness that lingered in the air.

It was in that moment, as Bella took her last breath, that Emma realized something she hadn't understood before. In the act of loving Bella, she had learned how to let go. She had held her through the pain, comforted her through the sorrow, and in return, Bella had taught her the true meaning of unconditional love—not just the kind that holds on, but the kind that knows when to release.

As Bella's body relaxed in Emma's arms, the first stars began to appear in the sky. Emma and Alex sat in silence, their hearts heavy, but their spirits lighter than they had been before. They had given Bella a home for her final days, and in return, she had given them the most precious gift of all: the ability to love without expectation and to say goodbye when the time came.

The porch, now empty, stood quiet in the fading light, the last sunset a bittersweet memory. But in the hearts of Emma and Alex, Bella's spirit would always remain, a reminder that love, even in its most painful moments, was never truly gone.

Echoes of the Past

Luna was more than just a service dog—she was a lifeline. For five years, she had been by Sarah's side, guiding her through the world with a sense of purpose that only a trained dog could provide. Sarah had been blind since birth, and Luna had become her eyes. The bond between them was unspoken yet profound. Sarah trusted Luna with her safety, her independence, and, most of all, her heart.

It was a crisp autumn morning when everything changed. Sarah and Luna were out on their usual walk through the park, Sarah holding tightly to Luna's harness as they navigated the familiar path. The sun was just rising, casting a golden glow across the trees, when the screech of tires shattered the quiet. Luna, ever vigilant, reacted instinctively, pulling Sarah away from the street just in time. But the car veered off course, hitting Sarah before she could fully get out of the way. The impact was instant, and Luna's world tilted.

In the aftermath, Luna was beside Sarah, who was unconscious on the ground. The sirens, the frantic voices, the chaos—it was all a blur. Luna stayed with Sarah through it all, her body rigid, her ears pressed flat against her head. But Sarah wasn't waking up.

The accident left Sarah in a coma for weeks, her condition critical. Luna was there every day, sitting by her side at the hospital, refusing to leave. But despite the doctors' best efforts, Sarah's injuries were too severe, and she passed away. Luna didn't understand. The woman who had given her purpose, who had loved her with a tenderness no one else could, was gone.

The days that followed felt endless for Luna. She was brought back to the quiet house, the one that had once been filled with Sarah's laughter, the sound of her gentle voice calling her name. But now, it was empty. The scent of Sarah lingered in the corners, but there was no one to reach out and call her. No one to give her commands. Luna spent her days wandering from room to room, her paws heavy with the weight of a grief she couldn't understand.

Sarah's family—her brother and his wife—tried to comfort Luna, but they were strangers to her. Luna had never spent much time with them, and though they were kind, their presence couldn't fill the void Sarah's absence had left. Luna resisted their attempts to bond, retreating to the corner of the house, longing for the familiar touch of her handler's hand on her head.

Weeks passed, and the family made a difficult decision. They couldn't keep Luna in the home—she needed more than they could give her. They contacted a local animal shelter that specialized in rehoming service dogs, hoping that Luna could find a new family who could care for her. The thought of letting go of Luna was heartbreaking, but they knew it was the best choice for the dog who had lost so much.

At the shelter, Luna was introduced to a new family—The Millers, a young couple with two children. They had recently adopted a boy named Ethan, who had autism, and they thought Luna could help him in ways that words never could. The Millers were kind and patient, but Luna couldn't shake the memory of Sarah. The new house felt strange. The children, though affectionate, felt like ghosts to her, too young to understand the depth of her pain.

Luna would often escape to the backyard, sitting by the old wooden fence and staring into the distance, her eyes clouded with longing. She didn't want to be here. She didn't want to leave Sarah behind. Every time Ethan tried to call her, Luna would hesitate, unsure of how to navigate this new life. It wasn't until one evening, when the family was having dinner, that something changed.

Ethan had been struggling with a sensory overload, his hands pressed to his ears as the noise in the house grew too much for him. Luna, who had been watching from the doorway, instinctively padded over to him. She nudged his hand gently with her nose, as if trying to offer him the same comfort she had once offered Sarah. Ethan looked up at her, his face scrunched with confusion, but then his expression softened. He reached out and placed his hand on her head, the warmth of his touch grounding Luna in a way she hadn't expected.

It was the first time Luna allowed herself to fully connect with Ethan. The pain of Sarah's loss was still there, lingering in the background, but Luna realized something in that moment. She wasn't replacing Sarah. She was carrying Sarah's spirit forward, offering the same love, the same support, to someone who needed it just as much.

From that night on, Luna found a new rhythm in her life. She would guide Ethan through the house, helping him navigate the world the same way she had once done for Sarah. The pain of loss never fully faded, but Luna learned that sometimes, the heart has room for more than one love. She could remember Sarah and carry her memory while still being there for Ethan, becoming the lifeline he so desperately needed.

And in the quiet moments, when the house was still, Luna would sit by the window and watch the sunset, a soft sigh escaping her as she thought of Sarah, feeling her presence not in the silence, but in the echoes of her past, whispering through the life she was living now.

Silent Guardian

Shadow had always been an invisible figure in the town, a stray dog who roamed the streets at night, sleeping in abandoned alleys and scavenging what little food he could find. He wasn't a pet, not really. His coat was matted, his ribs visible beneath his fur, and his eyes carried the weight of a thousand untold stories. But there was something about him—something quiet, something protective—that kept him from straying too far from the children who played in the park near his usual haunts.

It was in this park that he first noticed her—Maya, a small girl with dark brown eyes that held the sadness of someone much older than her ten years. She would often sit by the swings, clutching her books tightly to her chest as the other children teased her. Shadow would watch from the shadows, his keen eyes noticing how the other kids would laugh and whisper, never inviting her into their games. Maya would shrink into herself, her head bowed, her shoulders hunched as though she could shrink away from their cruel words.

Something about Maya's loneliness drew Shadow in. He began to appear more often, staying on the outskirts, just out of sight, watching as the bullies targeted her. He knew the pattern well—the taunts, the jeers, the way they made Maya feel small and invisible. It angered him, but he could do nothing—at least, nothing that would be seen. He was a stray, a nameless dog with no place in the world. But he wasn't helpless.

One afternoon, as Maya sat alone by the swings again, a group of older boys approached her. Shadow felt a familiar spark of anger. They were getting too close. Maya's hands gripped her book tighter, her face flushing with embarrassment. The boys started to circle her, laughing, pushing her around. Shadow could feel his muscles tense, the old ache in his body momentarily forgotten as he stepped out of the shadows.

Without a sound, Shadow lunged forward, his growl a deep rumble that stopped the boys in their tracks. The sudden presence of the large, shaggy dog was enough to send them scattering, their taunts turning into nervous laughter as they ran away. Maya sat frozen, her wide eyes staring at the dog who had saved her. Shadow stood tall, his body tense but watchful, his gaze never leaving the spot where the boys had just been.

Maya didn't move, not at first. She was stunned, unsure of what to do with the new presence in her life. Slowly, she reached out a trembling hand, and after a long moment of hesitation, Shadow took a step closer. He didn't need to be invited; he was already there. Maya gently placed her hand on his head, her fingers brushing through his tangled fur. She smiled softly, a small but real smile that reached her eyes for the first time in what seemed like forever.

From that day on, Shadow became her constant companion. He was always nearby, his presence like a silent shield against the world. Maya no longer sat alone in the park. She could still feel the sting of their words sometimes, but now, there was a steady warmth by her side, a silent guardian who stood between her and the cruelty of the world.

As the months went by, Maya noticed the change in Shadow. He had always been thin and scrappy, but now he seemed weaker. His coat, though thick and shaggy, was no longer as glossy. His movements were slower, his steps more labored. Maya could see it, the way he limped slightly as he walked, the way he sometimes struggled to climb the small hill to their favorite spot near the swings. But still, he never left her. He was always there, even when his health seemed to worsen. She could see the gray in his muzzle and the dullness in his eyes, but his spirit never wavered.

One particularly cold winter afternoon, Maya was sitting on the swings again, reading quietly when she noticed Shadow had not joined her. She looked around, her heart sinking as she stood up, calling his name. "Shadow?" Her voice trembled, the fear settling in her chest.

She hurried through the park, her breath quickening as she searched. Finally, she found him lying near the edge of the park, in the snow. His breathing was shallow, his body trembling with the effort it took just to stay awake.

Maya knelt beside him, tears welling in her eyes as she gently stroked his fur. "Please, Shadow," she whispered, her voice cracking. "Please stay with me."

Shadow's eyes flickered open, a small, tired smile tugging at his lips. He looked up at her with the same protective gaze he had always had, as though telling her that he had done his job. He had kept her safe, kept her from the worst of the world's cruelty. And now, it was time to rest.

With a final, deep sigh, Shadow closed his eyes. His body relaxed, his breaths slowing, until there was nothing left but the quiet, peaceful stillness of the snow around them.

Maya stayed with him until the last light of the day faded, her hand resting on his fur, the snow falling softly around them. Shadow had given her something no one else could—something far more valuable than just protection. He had given her the courage to face the world, the courage to believe that she was worth something. Even in his final moments, he had protected her from the pain of loneliness, just by being there.

The park grew quiet as the day ended, but Maya wasn't alone anymore. She knew she would carry the memory of Shadow with her always, a silent guardian who had taught her the strength of love, even when words were never spoken.

The Forgotten Friend

Charlie had always been the type of dog who trusted without question, loved without hesitation. He was a mixed breed, with patchy brown fur and soulful eyes that never stopped watching, never stopped hoping. He had been part of the Thompson family for six years, ever since he was a puppy. For most of that time, life had been good. The Thompsons—Rachel, Sam, and their two children, Lucy and Ben—had treated him like family. He had a warm bed by the fireplace, long walks in the park, and the constant companionship of a family who loved him.

But then, the hard times came.

It started with Sam losing his job, the bills piling up faster than Rachel could handle. The house that had once been filled with laughter began to echo with silence. The kids became quieter, their toys gathering dust in the corners of their rooms. Rachel worked long hours at a local café, Sam took odd jobs, but it was never enough. Tension built in the household, and the once cheerful Thompsons began to lose hope.

One morning, Charlie woke up to find that the family was gone—packed up and left without a word. He could smell the remnants of their presence, the lingering scent of Rachel's perfume, Sam's cologne, and the faint trace of the children's laughter in the air. But the house was cold and empty. The door was left ajar, and Charlie, confused and anxious, padded through the house, sniffing every corner, waiting for someone to return.

Hours turned into days, and still, there was no sign of them. The food bowl sat untouched, the leash still hanging by the door. Charlie stayed there for as long as he could, curled up on the couch where Rachel used to sit, staring out the window for any sign of his family. But as the days turned into weeks, hunger gnawed at his stomach, and loneliness crept into his bones.

Finally, when there was nothing left for him in the house, Charlie made the decision to leave. He didn't understand why his family had abandoned him, but he knew he couldn't stay there forever. Maybe they had gone somewhere else. Maybe he could find them, bring them back. His loyalty to them was unwavering, even if their loyalty to him had faded.

He set off into the world, his paws growing sore from the pavement, his coat thinning as the weather turned colder. Along the way, Charlie encountered both kindness and cruelty. An elderly woman with a soft heart gave him a meal and a warm blanket for the night, her hands trembling as she stroked his fur. "Where did they go, sweet boy?" she asked, her voice thick with sadness. But Charlie didn't have an answer.

Other times, he found no kindness at all. In the alleyways and streets, he was chased away by strangers who saw him as nothing more than a nuisance. A group of boys threw rocks at him, their laughter echoing in the empty streets as Charlie ran, his tail between his legs, trying to escape their jeers. But even in the face of cruelty, Charlie's heart remained open, his trust unbroken. He didn't know who had hurt him, but he believed there was good in the world somewhere, just as he had once believed in the goodness of his family.

As the weeks passed, Charlie grew weaker. His coat had become patchy, and his bones ached from the constant search. He had wandered far from home, and now, his once-bright eyes had dulled with exhaustion. He was tired, so tired, but he couldn't stop. The thought of finding his family, the thought of reuniting with them, kept him moving, kept him going.

One evening, as Charlie walked through a new neighborhood, he saw a small house with a warm glow coming from the windows. He approached cautiously, his nose twitching at the scent of food and warmth. He was so tired, and his paws hurt, but the smell was too inviting to ignore. He crept closer and saw a family inside—two children laughing, a man and a woman sitting at the table, sharing a meal.

Charlie hesitated for a moment, the memory of his own family flashing in his mind. But then the door opened, and a woman stepped out, holding a bowl of food. She looked at him, her eyes softening. "Oh, you poor thing," she murmured, her voice gentle. "Come here, let's get you something to eat."

Charlie took a tentative step forward, his stomach growling, and let her lead him into the warmth of the house. The woman, whose name was Sarah, sat with him as he ate, her hands gently petting him. "You must have been through so much," she said, her voice filled with empathy. "You deserve a home. A real home."

Charlie felt a sense of peace he hadn't known in weeks. For the first time since his family left, he felt safe again. The warmth of the house, the kindness in Sarah's eyes—it was everything he had been searching for. But as he lay down by the fire that night, his mind drifted back to the Thompsons. Had they forgotten him completely? Would he ever see them again?

The next morning, Sarah took Charlie to the vet, where they discovered he was much older than they had originally thought. His health was failing, and his heart was weak. The vet said he had little time left, but that didn't matter to Sarah. She loved him, and that was enough.

As the days passed, Charlie's health continued to decline. But in his final days, he found something he hadn't known he needed—someone who cared for him, who loved him not out of obligation, but out of choice. And though his time with Sarah was short, Charlie finally understood what it meant to truly be loved and cared for, not just as a pet, but as a companion.

In the end, Charlie never did find the Thompsons again. But he found a home where he was cherished, a place where he could rest and be at peace, knowing that even when the world had forgotten him, there were still some who would choose to remember.

Rainy Day Promises

The sound of rain drumming against the windows was the only thing that filled the silence in the small apartment. Eleven-year-old Luke sat on the edge of his bed, his knees pulled up to his chest, his head resting against his arms. The world outside was grey and heavy, mirroring the sadness that had taken root inside him. His parents' divorce had been final for just over a month, but the pain still felt raw, like an open wound that no amount of time could heal.

It wasn't just the absence of his mother or father that hurt. It was the quiet, the stillness that followed when they left him with his thoughts. He had learned to navigate the changes—the moving, the new routines, the different houses—but none of it felt right. The laughter he once shared with his parents had become strained and distant, replaced by whispered arguments, late-night silences, and the uncomfortable shifting of furniture that spoke of things being torn apart. His family was no longer whole.

One afternoon, as the rain continued to pour outside, Luke's father took him to the local animal shelter. It had been his idea, trying to distract Luke from the sadness that seemed to cloud him all the time. "Maybe a dog would help you feel better," his father had suggested, his voice tired and quiet, as if unsure of the best way to reach his son.

Luke wasn't sure if a dog could make him feel better, but he agreed nonetheless. The shelter smelled of disinfectant and loneliness, the rows of cages holding dogs who stared out with longing eyes. Some of them barked when they saw Luke, their tails wagging with hope, while others lay still, waiting for something—or someone—to change their fate.

It was in the back corner of the shelter that Luke first saw her. A medium-sized dog with a patchy coat, her fur damp from the humidity, was curled up on a small blanket. Her eyes, though weary, looked up at him with an intense gaze that seemed to speak without words. Her name was Rain, the shelter worker explained. She had been abandoned by her previous owners, and though she was friendly, she had been waiting for a family for months.

Luke knelt down, and Rain cautiously approached the bars of her cage, her ears perked as she sniffed the air around him. He reached his hand through the bars, and she nudged it gently with her nose. For the first time in weeks, Luke felt a warmth inside him—a connection to something that wasn't broken.

"She's been here too long," the worker said softly. "She's a sweet dog. She just needs someone to give her a chance."

Without a second thought, Luke turned to his father. "Can we take her home?" he asked, his voice barely above a whisper.

That afternoon, Rain became part of their family.

In the weeks that followed, Luke and Rain formed a bond that neither of them had expected. She was gentle, always there when he needed her—laying beside him as he read, following him around the apartment as if keeping him safe from the world. Rain's presence filled the empty spaces in the apartment, as if she, too, was trying to heal from the wounds of her past.

Whenever Luke felt overwhelmed by the chaos of his parents' divorce, he would sit on the couch, resting his head against Rain's soft fur, her warmth offering a comfort that words couldn't. He could talk to her about the things he couldn't bring himself to say to anyone else—the confusion, the anger, the sadness. Rain didn't judge him. She simply listened, her gentle eyes never leaving his face. In return, Luke gave her the affection and love she had been missing for so long, his hands stroking her coat with a tenderness he had forgotten he was capable of.

On rainy days, when the clouds seemed too thick to let the sun through, Luke and Rain would sit by the window, watching the world outside. The rain felt like a companion, always there, never judging, just falling with quiet persistence. As Luke's fingers traced the outline of

Rain's ear, he realized something—that maybe, in a way, they weren't so different after all. Both of them had been abandoned, left to figure out how to navigate a world that felt uncertain and cold. But in each other, they had found something to hold onto.

One afternoon, Luke sat quietly on the floor, watching as Rain curled up beside him, her head resting on her paws. His father had come to pick him up, and Luke's stomach twisted at the thought of leaving the small apartment, leaving Rain behind. It wasn't that he didn't want to go—it was just that he knew, deep down, he wasn't ready to let go of the one constant thing in his life.

As his father's voice called him from the other room, Luke walked over to Rain, his hand gently resting on her head. "I'll be back soon," he whispered, more to himself than to her. "I promise."

Rain looked up at him, her eyes filled with understanding. Then, she nudged him with her nose, her tail giving a soft wag as if to reassure him. Luke smiled faintly and walked toward the door, his heart heavy.

But when he turned to look back, he saw Rain still lying on the floor, her gaze never leaving him, her ears slightly perked in the way she always did when she was waiting. As the door closed behind him, Luke realized something—he wasn't the only one who needed a promise.

Rain had waited for him, and in her quiet, steadfast way, she was teaching him the value of staying, of waiting for things to get better, even when they seemed beyond repair. In a world that was broken and unsure, sometimes the only thing you could trust was the promise that someone, something, would always be there.

The rain continued to fall as Luke walked away, but for the first time in a long time, the world didn't feel quite so heavy.

Through Her Eyes

Molly had never known sight. From the day she was born, the world had been a blur of smells, sounds, and sensations. Her vision was a silent void, but it was never something she missed. She learned to navigate the world with her nose, her ears, and her paws. She knew the feel of the grass beneath her feet, the scent of the morning dew, and the comforting sound of her owner's voice calling her name. To Molly, life was full of vivid textures and rich scents—a world that needed no sight to appreciate.

Her owner, Emma, had always been her guide. Emma, a woman in her mid-sixties, had raised Molly from a puppy. Together, they had built a life filled with routines—morning walks, lazy afternoons on the porch, and evenings spent curled up together on the couch. Emma, though aging, had been strong and steady. She had always been Molly's eyes, her gentle hand guiding Molly through the house, showing her the world.

But as the years passed, something began to change. Emma's vision, once clear and sharp, started to blur. She had trouble reading the newspaper in the mornings, and soon, she could no longer see the faces of her grandchildren during visits. The doctor had said it was age-related macular degeneration, a condition that would only get worse with time. Emma fought the diagnosis at first, but the world around her grew increasingly hazy, and soon she found herself struggling to see even the most basic things—her own reflection in the mirror, the face of her beloved dog, Molly.

At first, Emma tried to continue with her daily life as usual. She used a cane when she went outside, clinging to the walls for guidance when she moved about the house. But each day, the world seemed to grow darker. Molly, always by her side, began to sense the change. The gentle nudges from Emma's hand, once filled with affection, now seemed less confident, more hesitant. Molly, though blind herself, could feel the tremors in Emma's steps, the way her owner faltered just a little more each time they crossed the room.

One quiet afternoon, as the autumn leaves rustled outside the window, Emma sat on the couch, her hand resting in Molly's fur. Her face was calm, but there was an unmistakable sadness in her eyes. Molly could sense it, the shift in Emma's energy. Molly nuzzled her gently, her nose brushing Emma's hand, trying to offer the comfort she had always received.

It was then that Emma whispered, "I don't know how much longer I can do this, Molly. I'm scared."

Molly's tail gave a small thump against the floor. She couldn't understand the words, but she understood the tone—the quiet sorrow, the confusion. She had always been the one to follow Emma, but now, it seemed as if Emma needed her in a way she had never needed before. Molly stood up and walked around the couch to Emma's side, nudging her gently, offering her warmth, her presence. She knew the familiar rhythm of Emma's hands, the way they would stroke her fur, and she waited patiently for Emma to find her, to hold onto her.

As the months passed, Emma's sight grew worse. She could no longer manage the simple tasks she had once done effortlessly—baking, reading, even picking out her own clothes. Molly, in turn, became more aware of Emma's vulnerability. She began to guide her in ways she hadn't before. When Emma reached out for something on the kitchen counter, Molly would nudge her hand toward it. When Emma stood at the door, unsure of where to step, Molly would press her body against Emma's leg, guiding her through the threshold. The roles had reversed in subtle ways, and Emma leaned on Molly more than she ever had.

It wasn't always easy. Emma's steps were slower, her movements more uncertain. Molly, once so independent in her own blindness, now found herself leading the way, watching carefully as Emma followed. There were days when Emma would stumble or miss the steps on the staircase, and Molly would stop her with a soft nudge, her tail low, her body tensed in concern. It was a quiet dance, a bond that needed no words.

One evening, as they sat on the porch, the sun sinking below the horizon, Emma asked softly, "How do you do it, Molly? How do you keep going, even when you can't see?"

Molly's ears perked up at the question, but she remained still, her eyes trained on Emma, even though she couldn't see her. The wind stirred the leaves, and the world was bathed in the last light of the day, a world both of them knew by touch and sound. Molly rested her head on Emma's knee, her body close, offering her warmth, her presence. Emma smiled, a bittersweet smile that tugged at Molly's heart. She didn't know how, but she understood the question.

As the days continued, Emma's condition worsened. She could no longer navigate the house alone. Her children and grandchildren came to visit, but it was Molly who stayed by her side, never leaving, always watching. Emma's health declined, and one night, as the house grew still, Emma lay in her bed, her breathing shallow. Molly lay at her feet, just as she had for so many years.

When Emma passed away, it wasn't in a grand moment, but in the quiet way they had lived together—the two of them, each dependent on the other, each offering the other love in ways that words could never capture. Molly stayed by Emma's side, her head resting on the blanket, until the final breath had passed.

In the days that followed, the house felt emptier. But as the rain began to fall one afternoon, Molly sat by the window, watching the droplets run down the glass. She could no longer see Emma, but she felt her presence in every corner of the house. In the same way Emma had once guided her through a dark world, Molly knew that she would carry the love and the memories of their bond with her, guiding her through the silence of the coming days.

Molly, the blind dog, had learned to see in a way no eyes could ever capture. Through the touch of a hand, the feel of a heartbeat, and the warmth of another soul beside her, she understood the world in a way that surpassed sight, a lesson that neither vision nor blindness could define. 23

Farewell to the Farm

Rusty had always known the farm as his world. The sprawling fields, the scent of fresh hay, the rhythmic sounds of the cows in the barn, and the occasional crowing of the rooster at dawn—it was his domain, his life. The Thompson family had brought him home as a puppy, and from the moment he stepped onto the farm, he knew he belonged. Rusty had always been a part of the rhythm of the farm: chasing the chickens back to the coop, rounding up the cows, and even napping beneath the porch as the sun beat down on the land. It was a life full of purpose, and he loved it.

But then, the storm came.

It wasn't a thunderstorm or something familiar. It was something far worse, something that rattled even the oldest barns and split the earth with an intensity Rusty had never known. The family had heard the warning on the radio, but no one expected the storm to come for them. By the time they could react, the tornado had already touched down, tearing through the fields and ripping apart the barn where Rusty slept most nights. The wind howled, the earth trembled, and in the chaos of the disaster, Rusty had been separated from the Thompsons.

When the storm had passed, the landscape was unrecognizable. The house was still standing, but much of the farm had been destroyed. The fields were flooded, the crops ruined, the barn reduced to rubble. Rusty found his way back to the farmhouse, his paws muddied and his coat damp from the rain, but when he arrived, he found the family packing up. They weren't staying. The damage was too much; the repairs too costly. They had made the difficult decision to leave the farm and relocate to the city, where they hoped life might be a little easier.

Rusty, standing in the doorway, watched them load the last of their belongings into the truck. He didn't understand. He wanted to follow them, to stay close to the people who had always been his pack, but the reality of the situation began to settle in. They weren't staying. He wasn't sure where he would fit in now that everything had changed.

The move to the city wasn't kind to Rusty. The Thompsons had arranged for him to stay with a family friend for a while, someone who could care for him until they found a more permanent solution. Rusty didn't want to go; he didn't want to leave the place he had known as home. But there was nothing he could do. His paws felt heavy as he followed the family friend, a kind woman named Alice, into the small apartment she lived in. The bustling city was a far cry from the quiet, wide-open spaces of the farm, and every street corner, every noisy honk of a car, felt foreign to Rusty. The apartment smelled different, the walls were too close, and the neighbors' voices were a constant reminder that life had moved on without him.

Days turned into weeks, and Rusty struggled to adapt. He missed the open fields, the familiar scent of the barn, the comforting presence of the Thompsons. Alice was kind to him, but she was busy with her own life, and Rusty often found himself wandering aimlessly around the apartment, his body restless and his mind confused. He'd sit by the window, watching the cars rush past, wondering where his family had gone. Why had everything changed?

One evening, as the sun dipped below the skyline, Rusty found himself standing on the small balcony of Alice's apartment, looking out over the city. His coat was starting to thin, the fur duller than it had been back on the farm. The city was loud, the sounds of voices and machinery a constant hum that grated against his ears. He closed his eyes and remembered the peace of the farm, the way the fields stretched endlessly before him, the sun warm on his back, and the smell of the earth beneath his paws.

But it was gone now. Everything he had known was gone.

Just as the weight of that loss seemed too much to bear, Alice's voice broke through the sadness. "Rusty," she called softly, stepping onto the balcony. "Come inside. It's getting late."

Rusty turned to look at her. She was standing with a plate of food in her hands, offering him something to eat, a small gesture that seemed too insignificant to fill the hole left by the farm. But as he walked back toward her, his body heavy with exhaustion, something inside him shifted.

Alice had never been his family, but she had been kind. She had opened her home to him when everything had changed. She had given him a place to stay when the farm had been lost. And though it wasn't the same, it was something. It was a new beginning, not in a place he had chosen, but in a place where he could still find a sense of home.

That night, as Rusty lay on a soft rug near the warmth of the radiator, he realized something he hadn't fully understood before. The farm had been home, but home wasn't just a place—it was the people who loved you, who cared for you, no matter where you were. Rusty couldn't bring the farm back, but he could make a new home here, with Alice, with the city that felt too loud and too fast, but where he was still loved.

And in the quiet of the apartment, with the sound of Alice's breathing steady beside him, Rusty finally closed his eyes, knowing that though the world around him had changed, his heart would always carry the love and warmth of the family who had given him everything—and that love, he realized, would never be taken from him.

Broken Collar

Toby had always been a dog full of spirit, even from the moment he was a small puppy. He loved to run across the fields, chasing after sticks and jumping through tall grasses. But one fateful day, when Toby was just a year old, an accident changed everything. A car, swerving to avoid a wild deer, struck him on the side of the road. The accident left him with a limp, and for the first time in his life, Toby felt like he wasn't the same dog. He couldn't run like he used to, couldn't chase after the birds in the yard or race the kids down the driveway. His once energetic and eager movements slowed, and the familiar pain in his leg followed him everywhere.

At first, Toby's family—the Harrisons—tried to make adjustments. They gave him special cushions for his bed, ensured that he had a soft, comfortable place to rest, and made sure he got enough love and attention. But Toby could sense the change in their behavior. While they were kind to him, they were often more concerned about his limitations than his well-being. Sometimes, his owner, Emily, would sigh softly when he struggled to keep up with her on walks. And his little brother, Sam, who had once loved playing fetch with him, began to spend more time inside, less interested in the games they used to share.

Despite his disability, Toby still wanted to prove that he could be a good dog, that he could be a protector, a companion. He still tried to follow Emily around the house, tried to be near Sam when the boy sat on the floor with his toys. But the pain from his leg often made it hard for him to keep up, and he spent more and more time resting in his favorite corner of the living room, watching the world around him from the safety of his bed. His collar, once bright and colorful, now hung loosely around his neck, its tag jingling whenever he shifted.

One night, a storm rolled in. The wind howled against the windows, and the sky flashed with the brilliance of lightning. Emily and Sam had already gone to bed, with the power flickering in the house, but Toby remained alert. His ears perked at the sounds outside—the sharp crack of thunder, the distant rumble of something bigger. Something about the storm didn't feel right. It wasn't just the sound of rain tapping against the windows or the trees swaying in the wind. There was something else. Toby's instincts kicked in.

He rose from his bed, his leg aching with every movement, but he pressed on, determined to warn his family. He limped to the door, sniffing the air, his heart racing. The wind was strong now, pushing against the house, shaking the windows. Toby knew that if something was wrong, he had to act quickly.

Suddenly, there was a loud crash. The back door of the house was blown open by the fierce winds, and with it, the family's backyard shed collapsed, sending debris tumbling into the yard. A piece of the shed's roof flew toward the house, narrowly missing the window where Sam had been playing earlier. Toby's heart pounded as he saw the danger, and he knew he had to do something.

Though his leg burned with pain, Toby hobbled toward Emily's room. He barked frantically, trying to wake her, but his voice was drowned out by the howling wind and the storm's deafening roar. He paced, his limp slowing him down, but he wouldn't stop. The storm was too dangerous. He had to protect them.

Toby finally managed to nudge the door open with his nose. He grabbed the sleeve of Emily's pajama shirt in his mouth and tugged, pulling her gently toward the hallway. Startled and half-awake, Emily followed him into the living room, where she saw the debris from the shed scattered across the yard. Her heart stopped as she saw the damage, and the realization hit her: the storm wasn't over, and it was much stronger than she had first thought.

"Sam!" Emily shouted, rushing toward the bedroom. Toby limped ahead of her, guiding her through the darkened house. He reached Sam's room first, and with a burst of adrenaline, he scrambled up onto the bed, nudging the boy awake. Sam, groggy and confused, looked at his dog with wide eyes as the storm raged on.

"Sam, get up! We need to move!" Emily urged. The storm was getting worse, and the wind was threatening to tear the roof off. Toby, despite his limp and the pain that was clearly overwhelming him, barked again and again, urging Sam to follow.

The family huddled together in the basement, the storm howling above them. Toby curled up at their feet, his body exhausted but proud. He had done it. Despite his limp, despite the challenges his body had thrown at him, Toby had kept his family safe. And though his collar was no longer the bright, colorful thing it once was, it still jingled softly as he lay there—reminding him that he had not been forgotten.

The storm passed, leaving behind a trail of damage, but no injuries. The Harrisons, shaken but safe, slowly emerged from the basement. Emily hugged Toby tightly, tears in her eyes.

"You did it, boy," she whispered, her voice full of awe. "You kept us safe."

Toby looked up at her, his tail wagging weakly. His leg still hurt, but in that moment, none of it mattered. He had found his worth. His limp hadn't defined him. He had proven that, even broken, he could be strong. Even without running or chasing, he had protected the family he loved—and in doing so, he had found the true meaning of loyalty.

And though his collar was worn and broken, it no longer mattered. Because Toby had shown that strength wasn't about how fast you could run or how perfectly you could move. Strength was about heart—and his heart was as big as the world.

Moonlight Memories

Stella had always been a dog of the night. Her coat, dark as the midnight sky, blended seamlessly with the shadows, and her eyes—sharp and alert—seemed to glow with the secrets the night held. For eight years, she had served as a night patrol dog, guarding the quiet streets of the city and keeping watch over the people who slept peacefully in their beds. She had been a part of something bigger than herself, a protector, a companion, and above all, a loyal servant to her handler, Officer Grant.

Grant was the one who had chosen her from the shelter all those years ago. He had seen something in Stella that no one else had—the determination, the silent strength, the steady loyalty that made her perfect for night patrol. She had been young then, eager to prove herself, and Grant had been patient, teaching her the ropes of their job. They had formed a bond over long nights of walking the empty streets, their silent companionship growing stronger with each step they took together.

Stella's memories of those early days were clear. The scent of rain on the pavement, the soft rustle of leaves in the wind, the distant hum of the city that never truly slept. There had been moments of quiet stillness, where it was just her and Grant, side by side, listening for any sign of trouble. They had caught thieves, helped lost children find their way home, and stood guard during the most uncertain hours of the night. Together, they had faced danger and darkness, always returning to the station as the first light of dawn broke over the horizon.

But that was all in the past now.

The streets were quieter these days. Stella's once sharp hearing had dulled, and her legs, which had once carried her swiftly through the night, now ached with every step. She had been retired from active duty a month ago, her age and health no longer suitable for the long nights on patrol. Grant had been there when she had been officially retired, his face a mixture of pride and sorrow. He had given her a final pat on the head and told her she had done more than enough, that she had earned her rest. But Stella couldn't help the emptiness that settled in her chest as he walked away, leaving her behind in a world she no longer understood.

Now, she spent her nights alone, lying in the corner of the small apartment she had once shared with Grant. The city still buzzed outside, the sounds of life continuing without her, but inside, the silence was deafening. Stella had tried to fill the empty space with the routines she had once known—laying in her favorite spot by the window, watching the moon rise over the city, but it wasn't the same. The nights felt longer, colder, without Grant by her side.

As the weeks passed, Stella's thoughts often wandered back to the adventures they had shared, to the nights filled with purpose and meaning. She could still remember the way Grant's voice had always reassured her, the way his hand had patted her head before each patrol. She had known what to do without question, had followed his lead without hesitation. Those were the nights when she had felt truly alive, when she had known her place in the world. But now, that world had changed.

One particularly quiet evening, as Stella gazed out at the moonlit streets from her spot by the window, a faint sound caught her attention. She stood up slowly, her joints aching, and padded toward the door. The street outside was as empty as it had always been, but something about the night felt different—almost as if it was calling to her. A memory flashed through her mind, a memory of her and Grant walking side by side, their steps in perfect sync, the world stretching before them, filled with endless possibilities.

Stella let out a soft whine, her ears perked, listening intently. It was an old instinct, the one that had guided her through countless nights of duty. She knew that there was something out there, something she couldn't ignore. With a final glance back at the empty apartment, Stella pushed open the door and stepped out into the cool night air.

She walked slowly at first, her body stiff with age, but as she moved through the streets, the familiar scents of the city seemed to awaken something within her. The smell of fresh rain on the pavement, the distant murmur of a passing car, the flutter of wings from a nearby rooftop—it all felt so familiar, so right. She had been here before, had walked these streets countless times with Grant by her side. But tonight, she was alone, and the weight of that loneliness was heavy.

As Stella made her way down the familiar path, a soft voice echoed in her memory—Grant's voice, steady and comforting. *"You've got this, girl."*

Suddenly, her body moved with purpose, her legs carrying her faster than they had in weeks. She followed the sound of muffled footsteps up ahead, moving closer, her instincts sharper than they had been in ages. She could hear the faint sounds of a struggle, a voice calling for help.

Without hesitation, Stella bounded toward the sound, her muscles straining as she pushed forward. Her heart pounded in her chest, not from fear, but from the sheer force of her determination. The moonlight shone brightly overhead as she reached the corner of the alley where the struggle was taking place. A man was holding a purse, trying to wrest it from a woman's grasp. Stella barked loudly, her voice carrying through the night.

The man turned in surprise, momentarily distracted, and the woman took the opportunity to break free. Stella lunged at him, her teeth bared, but instead of a confrontation, she simply stood her ground, her presence enough to send him running. He dashed off into the shadows, disappearing into the night.

The woman, now safe, looked down at Stella with wide eyes, her breath ragged. "Thank you," she said, her voice trembling. Stella gave her a soft bark, her tail wagging weakly before she turned and began her slow walk back toward home.

As Stella walked back toward her apartment, a sense of peace washed over her. She had done it, just like she always had. The moonlight cast a soft glow on her coat, and for the first time in weeks, Stella didn't feel quite so alone. She had remembered who she was, and what she was capable of. The years of patrols, the bond she had shared with Grant—they hadn't disappeared. They were still with her, guiding her, even in her retirement.

When she finally returned to the apartment, she lay down on her bed, her body weary but satisfied. She closed her eyes, and for a moment, the memories of her past adventures—of Grant, of the streets they had walked together—flooded her mind. And in that moment, Stella knew that, though she might be retired, her purpose was never truly gone. She had given all she had, and in the quiet of the night, she was reminded that sometimes, even in retirement, there is still room to answer the call.

The Long Wait

Diesel had never known a world without his owner, Nathan. The two had been inseparable since Nathan had brought him home as a puppy, just after his return from his first deployment overseas. Diesel, a strong and loyal Belgian Malinois, had been trained to protect, to watch, and to serve, but most of all, he had been trained to love, and that love was always focused on Nathan.

When Nathan had left for his most recent deployment, Diesel had been confused at first. Nathan had explained, his voice soft and reassuring, "I'll be back soon, buddy. Stay strong, Diesel. Protect the house." Diesel, his dark eyes full of trust, had watched his owner climb into the truck, his heart heavy with uncertainty, but Nathan's words gave him hope. It would only be a few months, just a few months of waiting. Diesel could do that. He had done it before.

The first few days after Nathan left were difficult. The house, which had once been filled with laughter and the sound of Nathan's voice, now felt cold and empty. Diesel paced the floors, his paws clicking on the hardwood, the silence unbearable. He would sit by the door, staring out the window, waiting for Nathan to return. His keen senses told him that Nathan had been gone for longer than usual, but he refused to believe it. His loyalty was absolute—Nathan would come back, just as he always had.

Days turned into weeks, then into months. Diesel would wait by the door in the evenings, his ears straining at the sound of car engines passing by, hoping to hear Nathan's truck pull up. When the doorbell rang, his heart would leap, only to deflate when it wasn't Nathan standing there. He would return to his spot by the window, looking out into the empty street, waiting, always waiting. His eyes, once bright with the vigor of youth, began to dull with time and longing.

Every morning, Diesel would get up, stretch his legs, and go to the door again. His routine remained steadfast, the same as the day before. He ate the food Nathan had left for him, took his walks, but everything felt wrong. Without Nathan, nothing felt right. The world had become an endless cycle of waiting, a quiet existence that felt like it was stretching on forever.

One day, the neighbor, Mrs. Anders, came over with a bag of treats. Diesel liked Mrs. Anders—she was kind, and sometimes she would play with him in the yard. But today, her face was solemn, her eyes filled with something that Diesel didn't quite understand. She knelt down beside him, running her hand over his back.

"Your dad's been gone a long time, hasn't he, Diesel?" she said softly, her voice trembling. Diesel looked up at her, his tail wagging a little, hoping that she might bring Nathan back. But Mrs. Anders didn't say anything else. She just hugged him gently, her eyes brimming with sadness. Diesel didn't understand why she was so upset. He thought she would know that Nathan would come home soon. He had to.

As the months continued to stretch on, Diesel grew older. His muscles were not as quick as they had once been, his steps a little slower. Yet still, he sat by the door every evening, watching the horizon, waiting for the familiar sound of Nathan's truck pulling up. The waiting had become part of him—his life was defined by it. Diesel didn't know how much longer he could keep this up, but he had no choice. He had promised Nathan that he would protect the house, that he would wait. And that was what he would do, no matter how long it took.

Winter came, and with it, the biting cold. Diesel's coat was thick, but the chill still seeped into his bones as he spent his nights by the window. The world outside was quiet, still, and white with snow. Diesel stared at the snowflakes falling, each one a reminder of how much time had passed. How much longer would it be? His body was tired, his paws aching, but still he waited. Every day, he waited.

Then one morning, the door opened unexpectedly. Diesel's ears perked up, and his heart raced. The scent of his owner—the scent that he had memorized, the one that had always brought him peace—was in the air. He leaped to his feet, his tail wagging furiously, ready to greet Nathan, to feel the comfort of his presence again.

But when he turned, his heart sank.

A man stood in the doorway, but it wasn't Nathan. The man was in a uniform, one Diesel had seen before—the same kind Nathan had worn during his service. The man knelt down and placed a hand on Diesel's head.

"Hey, boy," the man said softly. "I'm sorry. I'm so sorry. Your dad... he didn't make it back." His voice cracked, and Diesel could feel his chest tighten as the words settled around him.

The world around Diesel seemed to blur as the truth hit him. Nathan wasn't coming back. The promise of his return, the hope that had fueled every day, every hour of waiting, was gone. Diesel looked up at the man, his eyes full of confusion, unable to understand why Nathan wasn't there. The man's face was kind, but there was nothing he could say to undo the pain, to bring Nathan back.

Days turned into weeks, and the reality of Nathan's absence began to sink in. Diesel still waited by the door, though his heart was no longer full of hope. He still looked out the window, his eyes strained with longing, but the world was no longer the same. The house felt emptier than ever, the silence more overwhelming. Diesel had kept his promise—he had waited, but the waiting had no end.

And yet, as the seasons changed, as the years slowly passed, Diesel found something unexpected. The man in the uniform came by regularly, bringing food, water, and company. He would sit with Diesel, his hand resting gently on the dog's head, telling him stories about Nathan. About the days they had spent together, about how much Nathan had loved Diesel. And in those moments, Diesel realized something he hadn't understood before—the love that Nathan had given him, the loyalty they had shared, didn't disappear just because Nathan was gone. It lived on in the memories, in the stories that were told, in the bond that nothing could break.

Diesel didn't have to wait for Nathan to return. Because in a way, Nathan had never really left at all.

Winter's Embrace

Frost had never known warmth in the way most dogs did. His coat, thick and dense, was built for the harshest of winters, but even his strength couldn't ward off the cold that gnawed at his bones. He had been a part of the Martinez family since he was a pup, spending his early years chasing after sticks in the yard, basking in the sun, and curling up by the fire at night. But that was before things changed. Before the house grew quiet, the voices around him faded, and his family moved away without so much as a goodbye.

The Martinez house had sat abandoned for months, its windows broken, the door left ajar. Frost had no choice but to stay, guarding the empty space he once called home. As the weeks turned into months, the winter settled in, a harsh and unrelenting cold that wrapped the world in its icy grip. Frost's food had long since run out, and though he had once been an agile, energetic dog, his strength had been sapped by hunger and the long days spent outside.

One evening, as the snow began to fall heavier than usual, Frost felt the bite of the wind more sharply than before. His paws were raw from trudging through the snow, and his coat, once thick and protective, felt thinner with each passing day. He found a corner of the porch to curl up in, trying to shield himself from the worst of the cold, but it wasn't enough. The world seemed to close in around him, the cold air pressing against his fur, the quiet of the night amplifying his loneliness.

He had almost fallen asleep when he heard a voice—a soft, raspy voice, like the wind itself was speaking.

"You're cold too, aren't you, old boy?"

Frost's head shot up, his ears alert, and he growled low in his throat. He had learned to be wary, had grown used to the silence of the world around him, but the voice didn't sound threatening. It was gentle, almost comforting in its way.

A figure appeared from the shadows—an older man, hunched over, his face weathered by years of hardship. His clothes were ragged, and his steps were slow, deliberate, as if the weight of the world was on his shoulders. He looked down at Frost with tired eyes and a worn-out smile.

"You're not from around here, are you?" the man asked, kneeling down carefully, his hands trembling as he reached out to Frost. "I've seen a lot of dogs, but none like you. You've been through something."

Frost remained still, watching the man, not sure whether to trust him. But the cold was overwhelming, and as the man settled next to him, his body seemed to absorb some of the harshness of the winter night. Frost slowly moved closer, sensing no threat. He wasn't used to human contact anymore—he hadn't been touched in so long—but this man's presence felt oddly familiar, like the kindness Frost had once known.

The man chuckled softly, rubbing Frost's fur with a gentleness that surprised the dog. "I don't have much," he said, looking up at the empty house. "But I've got this," he added, pulling a tattered blanket from a bag slung over his shoulder. "Not much to keep the cold away, but it's better than nothing."

Frost let out a soft whine as the man draped the blanket over him. The warmth from the blanket, and the man's touch, felt like the first sign of comfort Frost had known in a long time. It was a small act, but to the dog, it meant the world. For the first time in months, he felt a little less alone, a little less cold.

The man spoke again, his voice barely above a whisper. "I don't have anywhere to go either," he admitted, his gaze distant. "Been out here for... longer than I care to remember. But maybe we can keep each other warm tonight, huh?"

The two of them—Frost and the man—sat there in the growing snowstorm, side by side. The man's breath came in visible puffs, but he didn't seem to mind. He seemed content, even in his worn-out state, to share this moment with Frost. And Frost, who had never known companionship outside of his family, felt a connection he hadn't realized he was missing.

For the first time in months, the cold didn't feel so unbearable. The man's presence, though nothing like the warmth of the home he had once known, offered a kind of solace that Frost had forgotten existed. And as the snow continued to fall around them, they both drifted off into a light sleep, two lost souls finding warmth in the midst of winter's embrace.

But the next morning, when Frost woke up, the man was gone. The blanket remained, but the warmth was no longer there. The street was empty, the snow having buried everything in its wake. For a moment, Frost felt the familiar pang of loneliness. The man had disappeared into the city's shadow, just like so many people had disappeared from his life. But Frost knew that something had changed in him, something more lasting than the brief moment of warmth they had shared.

The winter was still cold. The house was still abandoned. But for the first time, Frost understood that sometimes, warmth isn't about where you sleep or how much you have. Sometimes, it's about the fleeting moments of connection that stay with you, even when everything else feels like it's slipping away.

And as Frost stood up, his paw prints leaving tracks in the fresh snow, he knew that, despite the world's coldness, there would always be room for one more memory—one more act of kindness—to carry with him through the winter's long embrace.

Silent Tears

Shadow had always been the dog who could sense what others couldn't. His thick, sleek fur and soft, understanding eyes made him the perfect companion for his job as a therapy dog. Trained to comfort those in pain, Shadow had been there for children who faced illness, loneliness, and sadness, providing the kind of quiet, unconditional support that only a dog could give. But for all the lives he had touched, Shadow had never quite met a heart as broken as that of Lily.

Lily was ten years old, with wide, brown eyes that held a deep, unspoken sorrow. She had been brought to the therapy center a few months ago, following the death of her parents in a car accident. The news had come like a lightning strike, sudden and shattering. Her aunt, her only remaining family, had brought her to live with her in a small town, but no one could fill the gap left behind by the loss of Lily's parents. She no longer laughed or played with her old friends; she spent most of her days withdrawn, staring out the window or sitting silently in the corner of the living room.

At the therapy center, Lily had been distant with everyone. The counselors had tried to talk to her, but her answers were short, her eyes always vacant. She wasn't angry. She was just empty. The grief had hollowed her out, and no one seemed to know how to reach her.

When Shadow was introduced to Lily, he noticed her immediately. He had been used to working with children who were struggling, but something about Lily's stillness made him pause. He sat beside her quietly, his black coat blending into the shadows, his eyes watching her with a mixture of patience and understanding.

Lily didn't look at him at first. She stared at the floor, her small hands curled tightly in her lap. But after a few minutes, Shadow's soft breathing and the warmth of his presence began to draw her attention. Slowly, she lifted her head. Her eyes met Shadow's, and for a brief moment, she seemed to see something in him—something safe. She reached out a tentative hand and touched his fur, her fingers trembling. Shadow didn't move, didn't nudge her or jump up. He simply stayed beside her, his body still, his presence unwavering.

The first days of their sessions were quiet. Lily would sit with Shadow, barely speaking, but the dog never seemed to mind. It wasn't about words; it was about the silence they shared, the mutual understanding that neither of them needed to explain the heaviness in their hearts. Lily would sometimes cry quietly, her shoulders shaking as the tears fell, but she never spoke of what hurt. Shadow would rest his head on her lap, his eyes always kind, always patient. He didn't force anything from her. He just let her be, and in doing so, Lily began to find a small measure of comfort.

Days turned into weeks, and slowly, Lily started to open up. She would bring her drawings to the sessions, pictures of her parents—small, happy moments frozen in time. In these drawings, Lily had captured what she couldn't say, her sorrow drawn with careful strokes of pencil and crayon. Shadow would sit beside her as she worked, his quiet companionship offering a sense of peace she hadn't known since the accident. She no longer felt like she was alone with the weight of her grief.

One afternoon, as the sun dipped low in the sky, Lily sat on the therapy center's porch with Shadow by her side. Her aunt had come to pick her up, but for now, it was just the two of them. Shadow lay with his head resting on Lily's feet, and she absentmindedly stroked his fur, her thoughts far away.

"You know," Lily whispered, almost to herself, "I keep waiting for them to come back. My mom and dad. I keep thinking maybe... maybe they'll come through the door one day. I'll hear them laughing, and I'll know everything's okay again." Her voice wavered slightly, but she didn't pull away from Shadow. "But they never come. And I don't know how to stop waiting."

Shadow raised his head, meeting her gaze with understanding, his dark eyes full of empathy. He leaned forward and placed a gentle paw on her knee. Lily looked down at him, the weight of her words hanging between them.

"I miss them," she added, her voice barely above a whisper. "I don't know how to be okay without them."

For the first time in months, Shadow gave a soft, almost imperceptible whine. It wasn't a call for attention, but rather an acknowledgment. Shadow understood what Lily couldn't say—that grief wasn't something that could be fixed. It wasn't something that went away. It wasn't something to "get over." It was something to live with, something that would always be a part of her, but not something that had to define her.

Lily's hand trembled as she continued to stroke Shadow's fur, the silence between them growing more comfortable, more familiar. Her tears had stopped for now, but the ache remained. Shadow didn't have the answers. He couldn't bring her parents back, couldn't erase the pain, but in that moment, he didn't need to. What he gave her wasn't a solution—it was space. Space to feel what she needed to feel, to cry if she needed to cry, to heal at her own pace. And as Shadow sat beside her, patiently waiting, he offered something that words could never express: the simple, healing power of presence.

When Lily's aunt arrived later, Shadow followed them to the car, his tail wagging softly. He had done his job for the day, but there would be other days, other moments, when Lily would need him again. As she climbed into the car, she glanced back at the dog who had helped her in ways she couldn't yet put into words. And though she still felt the ache of missing her parents, there was something different now. She was not as alone as she had been before.

In time, Lily would learn that grief wasn't something to be "fixed" or "solved," but something to carry, to heal from, and sometimes, just sometimes, something to share with a silent companion who understood.

The Final Fetch

Buddy had always loved the game. The sound of the ball bouncing across the grass, the thrill of the chase, the wind rushing past his ears as he leapt to catch it mid-air—it was the joy of his youth. He had been a sprightly pup when he first met Sarah, her face lighting up in delight the first time he caught the ball she threw. She had laughed, a sound that Buddy had come to recognize as his cue to run, his cue to give his all.

Now, at eleven years old, Buddy's joints creaked and ached with each step. His muzzle had grayed, and his once bright eyes were clouded with age. The fetches were slower, the jumps not as high, but Buddy still had that spark. He still had the will to try.

It had been a week since Sarah had returned from the vet, her face tight with worry as she looked down at Buddy. The doctor had told her that Buddy's heart was beginning to slow down, his body no longer the agile machine it once was. He was aging faster than Sarah was ready to admit. They'd talked about the "end of the road," as Sarah put it, but Buddy didn't fully understand what that meant. He just knew that Sarah had been sad, and that there had been a lot of quiet moments between them, when she simply petted him, speaking soft words he didn't entirely catch.

But one morning, something changed. Sarah picked up his favorite ball, the bright orange one Buddy had carried around for years. She tossed it gently onto the lawn, and Buddy's ears perked up at the familiar sight.

"Come on, Buddy," Sarah called softly, her voice tender but with a note of hope. "Let's go for one last run."

Buddy wagged his tail, though slower than before, and padded out to the yard. The grass beneath his paws felt cool and soft, and for a moment, he allowed himself to remember the days when running felt effortless. But despite the weariness in his bones, Buddy's heart stirred at the thought of chasing the ball again.

Sarah threw the ball gently, watching as it bounced just a few feet ahead of him. Buddy's first attempt to chase it was slow—his legs weren't what they once were—but there was no hesitation. His determination, as strong as it ever had been, propelled him forward. He felt the breeze rush past him, his ears flopping as he shuffled forward with all the energy he could muster. He reached the ball, pushing his aging body through the motion, and grabbed it in his mouth.

A small, triumphant bark escaped him as he turned back toward Sarah, tail wagging weakly. The happiness in his chest was unmistakable, his heart beating stronger in those brief, fleeting moments.

"Well done, Buddy," Sarah whispered, her voice thick with emotion as she knelt down to take the ball from him. "You're still my champion."

She threw the ball again, this time a little further. Buddy's steps faltered, but he pushed on, motivated by the connection between them, the bond that had carried them through countless walks, fetch games, and quiet evenings together. He reached the ball once again, slower now, his energy nearly gone, but still determined.

Sarah watched him, her heart breaking as she saw the weariness in Buddy's movements, but also the pure joy that radiated from his face. She knew this would be the last time they played this game together, that soon, he wouldn't be able to chase the ball at all. But for now, she wanted to give him one more moment, one more chance to feel the rush of the chase, to know the joy that had been such a big part of their life together.

As Buddy returned with the ball, Sarah's eyes filled with tears. She bent down and hugged him close, the ball falling softly to the grass between them. "I love you, Buddy," she said quietly, her voice choked with emotion. "I'm so proud of you."

Buddy lay down next to her, the ball forgotten. He rested his head on her lap, feeling the warmth of her hands as they ran through his fur. The joy of the game had faded, but the love they shared remained. He wasn't tired because he had failed; he was tired because he had given his all, as he always had. And now, in this quiet moment, surrounded by the world he knew, Buddy understood that his time with Sarah didn't have to be about the chase. It wasn't the ball, the run, or the fetch that mattered—it was the moments like these, where they were simply together, and he could feel the depth of their bond.

As the sun began to dip behind the trees, casting long shadows across the lawn, Sarah gently lifted Buddy into her arms, cradling him as she stood. She walked with him back to the house, the weight of the moment pressing heavily on her heart.

Buddy had given her more than just companionship—he had given her joy, unconditional love, and the kind of friendship that only a dog could offer. And in that final game of fetch, as Buddy lay his head against her chest, Sarah realized that the end wasn't just about saying goodbye. It was about cherishing the moments they had, the quiet, simple moments, and the love that would remain even when the game was over.

Buddy's last fetch had been the most perfect of them all, not because he had caught the ball or run the fastest, but because he had done it with all the love in his heart—and Sarah had been there to witness it.

Lost and Found

Scout had always been a dog of comfort, of routine. From the moment he was brought into the Mitchell family's home, his world had been small but safe. He had his own corner of the living room, his favorite blanket by the door, and the reassuring sound of his owner's voice, always calling him with warmth and affection. He had known every inch of the yard, every route they walked, every car that passed by the house. Life had been simple and predictable, and for Scout, that was enough. He was happy.

But that all changed the day the moving boxes appeared.

At first, Scout didn't understand what was happening. The Mitchells had been packing for days, filling the house with cardboard boxes and tape, their movements hurried and stressed. Scout watched them, his tail wagging at first, unsure of what it meant. But as the day wore on, the familiar scents in the house began to fade, replaced by the strange smell of bubble wrap and unfamiliar packing peanuts. There was a tension in the air that Scout couldn't ignore.

On the morning they were to leave, everything seemed off. The door was left open for a moment as Mrs. Mitchell ran back into the house to grab one last thing. Scout, curious as always, darted out the door, his paws quick on the pavement. He hadn't been outside much lately with all the moving, and the fresh air felt exciting, even though he wasn't supposed to be out there.

The world outside was big, so much bigger than the yard he had always known. Scout's nose twitched, and he started to trot down the street, his paws soft on the asphalt. He thought he'd just explore for a minute, maybe find a familiar face. But as he turned the corner, the door slammed shut behind him, and the sound startled him. He turned back quickly, but the house was gone. The car was gone. The Mitchells were gone.

His heart began to race.

He paced in front of the house, waiting for them to come back. But hours passed, and no one returned. It was as if the world had swallowed them whole. Scout's confusion turned to worry, and then to desperation. He ran up and down the street, barking, looking for anyone who might recognize him, but the city had changed in a way he didn't understand. There were so many smells, so many people, and none of them were his family.

As the sun began to set, Scout realized the enormity of his situation. He was lost.

The first night alone was the hardest. His stomach growled from hunger, and his paws ached from running. He found shelter under a bus stop, curling up in the corner, his head resting on his paws. He missed the warmth of his family, the comfort of his bed, and most of all, he missed the certainty that they would always come for him. He closed his eyes, hoping for sleep, but the uncertainty of the night kept him awake.

For the next few days, Scout wandered through the city, navigating its busy streets and unfamiliar alleyways. People would stop to look at him—some would smile and pet him, others would ignore him completely. He found food in scraps left behind by vendors, but it wasn't enough. He was always hungry, always searching for something that might lead him back home.

He remembered the park where the Mitchells used to take him, a place with a big oak tree in the center. He thought if he could just get back to the park, maybe he could find his way home. But the city was so vast, and the streets so confusing, that each day felt like he was getting farther from where he needed to be.

Days turned into weeks. Scout's fur grew matted and dirty, his body thinner than before. His steps had slowed, and the pain in his paws grew worse. He was tired, so very tired. But the thought of his family, the warmth of the house they had shared, kept him going. He couldn't give up. He had to find them.

One afternoon, while searching for food in a trash can, Scout heard a familiar voice. It was soft at first, but unmistakable.

"Scout? Scout?"

His heart leapt in his chest, and he turned toward the sound of his name. There, standing at the edge of the alley, was Mrs. Mitchell. Her face was tired, and there were tears in her eyes, but her voice was filled with joy as she called his name again. Scout's legs moved before he could stop them, and he rushed toward her, his tail wagging weakly.

She crouched down as he reached her, her arms wrapping around him tightly. "Oh, Scout," she whispered through her tears. "I've been looking everywhere for you. I'm so sorry. I didn't mean to leave you behind."

Scout licked her face, his heart filled with both relief and exhaustion. He had found her. He had found his family.

They sat together on the sidewalk for a long while, Mrs. Mitchell holding him close, her hands trembling. Scout didn't care that the city was loud around them, that the noise of passing cars and people echoed through the streets. All that mattered was that he was with her again.

But as Mrs. Mitchell stood to take him home, Scout hesitated. The streets were still so vast, the world still so big. He knew they would go back to a new place, a new home. But he also knew that, no matter where they went, the world would still feel a little less certain, a little more unfamiliar.

In that moment, Scout realized that no matter how far he had traveled or how lost he had been, the journey wasn't just about finding his way home. It was about the resilience to keep searching, even when hope seemed lost. It was about never giving up on the love and bond that had brought him this far.

And so, as Mrs. Mitchell led him back through the bustling streets, Scout walked with a quiet determination, knowing that the road ahead would be different, but the love he shared with his family would always be his guide.

Ashes to Ashes

Smokey had always been more than just a dog. He had been trained to help, to serve, and most of all, to protect. With his dark coat of fur, almost the color of smoke itself, he had been a natural fit as a rescue dog for the city's fire department. His handler, Lieutenant Sam Callahan, had been the one who had chosen him from the shelter, seeing not just the physical strength and sharp senses in the dog, but the potential for something deeper. They had made a formidable team, responding to call after call, saving lives together.

The sirens would wail, and Smokey would spring into action, racing alongside Sam as they ran toward the burning buildings, the crackle of flames rising around them. Sam's commands were always clear, and Smokey would follow, his eyes fixed on his handler's every movement. Together, they navigated the smoke and chaos, finding survivors, guiding them out of harm's way, and saving people from the jaws of danger. Smokey had never thought twice about it—he had a purpose, a mission, and he was proud to be part of the team.

But then came the fire that changed everything.

It had started as a routine call, a building fire on the edge of town. Nothing they hadn't dealt with before. Smokey had been ready, alert, and eager to help, as always. The flames had been roaring when they arrived, the building engulfed in smoke. The heat had been intense, but Sam had remained calm, as he always did. Smokey had worked alongside him, finding a trapped family on the second floor, guiding them down the stairs and out of the building. He had felt the satisfaction of completing their mission—people were safe, and that was all that mattered.

But as they went to exit, the building's structure began to give way. A loud crack filled the air, and before Smokey could react, a part of the ceiling collapsed directly over Sam. The explosion of debris had knocked Smokey back, sending him tumbling across the floor. He had heard Sam's voice, calling out, but when he tried to reach him, he found only more smoke, more debris, and nothing but the burning, choking smell of destruction.

The paramedics had come quickly, but it was too late. Sam was gone.

The loss of Sam was something Smokey couldn't process at first. He didn't understand why his handler wasn't there to give the next command, to pet him gently and tell him how proud he was. The firehouse felt empty without Sam's reassuring presence. Smokey had always been the one to guide people to safety, but now, he was the one who needed saving. The firehouse was still filled with the sounds of alarms, the clanging of boots, and the rush of firefighters, but it was all different now. Nothing felt the same without Sam.

Days turned into weeks, and Smokey found himself wandering the empty halls of the firehouse, the spot where Sam's boots used to be left by the door now vacant. He had no purpose. The calls came, but Smokey hesitated, unsure of his place. His heart wasn't in it anymore. The firehouse had always been a place of safety and camaraderie, but now, it was just another place of sorrow.

One evening, as Smokey lay in the corner of the firehouse, the doors opened, and a familiar face appeared. It was Sarah, Sam's daughter. She had been just a little girl when Smokey had first joined the crew, but now she was older, standing tall and proud in a firefighter's uniform of her own.

"Hey, boy," she said softly, her voice thick with emotion as she knelt beside Smokey. "You miss him, don't you?" Smokey didn't move, but he let out a soft whine, his head resting against her knee. Sarah stroked his fur, just as Sam had once done. "I miss him too," she murmured.

For the first time in weeks, Smokey felt a small flicker of something—perhaps it was hope, or maybe just the feeling of being needed again. Sarah stood up slowly, looking over at the fire engine parked in the bay. "You've been through so much, haven't you?" she asked. Smokey looked up at her, his eyes soft. "But you're still here, and I need you. I think Dad would have wanted you to stay."

The next day, Sarah took Smokey with her on a call. It was a small house fire, nothing too dangerous, but enough to get Smokey moving again. As they entered the house, Sarah led the way, with Smokey just behind her. It wasn't the same without Sam, but it was enough. Smokey's instincts kicked in once more, and though his body was older and slower, his heart was still in it. They cleared the house of smoke, found the trapped occupants, and got them to safety. As they walked back to the firetruck, Smokey felt something he hadn't felt in months—a sense of purpose. He had a new partner now, a new handler. Sarah wasn't Sam, but she was family, and that was enough.

Days turned into weeks, and Smokey began to feel himself healing, bit by bit. He wasn't the same dog he had been, not without Sam by his side, but he still had the fire inside him—the need to help, to protect, and to serve. Sarah took him on calls, and together they made a great team. Smokey had lost one handler, but he had gained another, and slowly, he began to find peace in that.

One evening, as Smokey lay by the firehouse door, the scent of smoke still lingering in the air, Sarah sat beside him. She reached down and stroked his fur, just as her father had done all those years ago. "You've been through a lot, haven't you?" she whispered, looking out over the horizon. Smokey rested his head on her lap, his eyes soft. He had lost much, but in finding Sarah, he had found a new purpose—one that, though different from the past, was still meaningful.

And as the firehouse continued its work, Smokey knew that though he would never forget Sam, there was still work to be done. The flame of courage still burned inside him, and he would carry it forward, one rescue at a time, with Sarah by his side.

In the end, Smokey realized that while grief could never be erased, it could be carried forward, like the embers of a fire that, when tended to with care, could still glow with warmth and light.

A Silent Goodbye

Grace had always been a quiet dog. From the moment she was born, the world had felt different for her. Sounds were distant, muffled, or simply absent altogether. She had never known the joy of hearing her owner's voice calling her name, or the comforting rhythm of footsteps approaching. Grace's world was one of touch and sight, of vibrations and gestures, of unspoken bonds.

Her owner, Emily, had known this from the very beginning. When she adopted Grace from the shelter, she didn't hesitate. Emily had always understood that love didn't need words, and she had never thought twice about adopting a dog who couldn't hear. Their bond was instant. Emily learned to communicate with Grace through hand signals, gentle touches, and the subtle way she understood her dog's every expression.

The house had always been filled with warmth. Emily would often catch Grace watching her, eyes full of understanding, tail gently wagging. They didn't need sound to communicate; they had perfected the art of silence. Their days were filled with simple routines—morning walks, afternoon naps, and evenings spent curled up on the couch, Emily reading her books as Grace rested her head on her lap, content in the quiet companionship.

But then, one day, Emily started feeling different. It began subtly at first—a little more tired than usual, a lingering ache in her chest, a sense of heaviness that wouldn't go away. She didn't tell Grace, not at first. She didn't want to worry her loyal companion, but soon the fatigue became overwhelming. Emily went to the doctor, and the diagnosis was swift and devastating: terminal cancer.

The news hit Emily hard, but it was Grace who seemed to know before the words were even spoken. Her dog had always been attuned to her emotions, sensing when Emily was upset or unwell long before she voiced it. In the days that followed, Emily could feel Grace's presence more keenly than ever. The dog stayed close, curling up beside her at all times, her warm body a steady comfort against the anxiety and fear that plagued Emily's thoughts.

Despite the heavy silence, Emily spoke to Grace every day, even though she knew her dog couldn't hear her. Her voice was soft, almost a whisper, and Grace would always look up at her, eyes filled with affection and understanding. Emily continued to give Grace the same care and attention she always had, taking her on walks, feeding her, and making sure to give her the best of everything, even as the world around her seemed to crumble.

The days grew shorter, and the illness took its toll on Emily. She grew weaker, the weight of the disease a constant, heavy presence. And still, Grace stayed by her side, never far away. She was always there—her silent, steady support offering Emily more comfort than any words ever could.

One cold winter evening, as the wind howled outside, Emily sat in her favorite armchair, wrapped in a blanket. Grace lay at her feet, her head resting on Emily's lap. The house was quiet, save for the occasional crackle of the fire in the hearth. Emily ran her fingers through Grace's fur, tears quietly streaming down her face as she whispered the things she had never said before.

"I'm sorry," Emily whispered, her voice breaking. "I'm sorry for leaving you. I don't want to go. You've been such a good girl, Grace. I wish I could stay."

Grace didn't move, but Emily could feel the weight of her dog's presence. It was as if Grace understood, even without sound, that time was running out. Emily's hand gently rested on Grace's back, her fingers tracing the lines of fur, as if committing the feel of her dog to memory.

The following days passed in a blur. Emily's energy dwindled, her body failing her despite her strength of spirit. Grace stayed close, never leaving her side. At night, when Emily would drift in and out of sleep,

Grace would nuzzle her gently, her warmth a comforting reminder of the love they shared. There was no need for words, no need for sound. Grace's devotion was enough.

One morning, Emily woke to find that her body was too weak to rise. She looked down at Grace, who lay beside her, her eyes full of understanding. Grace gently licked Emily's hand, her tail wagging once, as though to reassure her. Emily smiled faintly, her fingers moving to Grace's head as she whispered, "I'll always be with you."

And with that, Emily closed her eyes, her final breath soft and peaceful. Grace stayed by her side, her eyes unwavering, her silent presence offering the kind of comfort that transcended words.

Later that day, Emily's family arrived, but Grace had already known. She had sensed the shift, felt the absence, and in that quiet moment, Grace knew that her owner had gone. She had lost her best friend, the person who had loved her unconditionally, the one who had always been there.

But as Grace lay beside Emily's body, she felt no fear. She had given all the love she could, and in return, she had been loved in ways that words could never express. Her tail wagged softly, once more, in remembrance of a bond that was not bound by sound but by something far stronger.

Grace didn't need to understand the concept of goodbyes. She had loved, and been loved, without words, and that was enough. The silence between them was never empty. It had always been full of meaning.

And in the quiet that followed Emily's passing, Grace knew that the love they shared would remain with her, as silent and steadfast as the bond that had held them together.

Tears in the Rain

Rain had always loved the water. From the moment he was a pup, he had been drawn to lakes, rivers, and oceans, the rippling waves a constant source of joy and comfort. It was no surprise, then, when he became a water rescue dog. His thick, muscular frame, sleek coat, and natural ability to swim made him the perfect candidate. From his first days of training, he knew his purpose was to help, to save, and to be there for those in need, whether they were stranded on a riverbank or caught in a storm.

For five years, Rain had served alongside his handler, Lieutenant Olivia Harris. She had trained him, trusted him, and become his closest companion. Together, they had saved countless lives. Rain remembered each rescue vividly—the elderly woman clinging to a piece of driftwood as the current pulled her under, the young boy stranded on an inflatable raft in the middle of a choppy river, and the family whose boat capsized in a storm. Rain had been there for them all, pulling them from the water, keeping them safe, and bringing them back to shore.

But not every rescue had a happy ending. The memory that haunted Rain most was one that he could never erase from his mind. It had been a cold winter evening when a severe storm hit. The waves were furious, the winds howling, and the water choppy. A car had veered off the road and plunged into a freezing lake. Olivia had shouted commands, guiding Rain to the scene, the adrenaline rushing through their veins. He had plunged into the icy waters, instinctively following Olivia's instructions to find the car and bring out any survivors. He found one person, unconscious but alive. But there were others—two children, still in the car.

He remembered the feeling of his paws slipping on the slick surface as he tried to reach the car, trying to pull the children out, but the current was too strong. The storm raged on, and Rain was forced to retreat, helpless as the lake claimed the lives of those two children. The weight of the loss pressed on his chest, gnawing at him with every passing day.

Rain had never been the same since that rescue. He continued to serve, but there was a distance in his eyes that wasn't there before. Olivia noticed it too. She would often find him staring out over the water, as if searching for something he had lost. Sometimes, she would sit beside him, placing a hand on his head, offering him the kind of comfort that words could not express. She understood him in a way that no one else did. But even Olivia couldn't help him forget the trauma that lingered beneath the surface.

After the stormy night, the calls for rescues came less frequently, and eventually, the decision was made that Rain would retire. Olivia had been reluctant at first. He was still strong, still capable, but the trauma was evident in the way Rain looked at the water now—no longer with joy, but with sorrow and hesitation.

"I think it's time, boy," Olivia whispered one evening, as they watched the sun set over the calm waters. "You've given everything you had. It's time for you to rest."

And so, Rain retired. The days of rushing into the water to save lives were behind him, and now he spent his time in quiet solitude. He would still swim occasionally, but now, it was different. The water no longer felt like a friend—it felt like a reminder of the pain he had witnessed, the lives he could never save. The joy was gone.

Months passed, and the seasons changed. Olivia had found a new rescue dog, one younger and full of energy, and Rain watched from a distance as they trained together. He knew it was the right thing, that his time had passed, but it didn't make the emptiness inside him disappear. He couldn't shake the feeling that he was somehow incomplete.

Then, one stormy evening, as rain poured down in sheets and the wind howled outside, Olivia came to find Rain. She had been looking for him for hours, growing worried as the storm intensified. When she finally found him, he was standing at the edge of the lake, his coat wet from the downpour, his gaze fixed on the churning waters.

"Rain," Olivia called softly, her voice filled with concern. "What are you doing out here?"

Rain didn't answer, but his eyes—those deep, soulful eyes—turned to her. There was something in them, something that wasn't there before. A softness. A kind of understanding. Olivia stepped closer, sensing that Rain had come to a realization.

"You don't have to carry this burden alone anymore," she said, kneeling beside him, her hand gently resting on his back. "You've done your part, Rain. It's okay to let go now. You saved so many lives... you gave your heart to them. But you don't have to carry the weight of the ones you couldn't save."

Rain took a deep breath, his chest rising and falling slowly as the rain fell around them. He didn't need words to understand what Olivia meant. He had carried the guilt, the grief, and the sorrow for so long. It had become a part of him, but maybe, just maybe, it was time to stop holding onto it so tightly.

The storm raged on, but for the first time in a long while, Rain felt a sense of peace. He stepped into the water, the cold waves lapping at his paws, but he no longer hesitated. He swam through the water with a sense of release, as if the weight he had been carrying for so long was finally starting to lift.

Olivia watched him from the shore, her heart heavy with emotion but filled with a quiet understanding. She didn't need to tell him that he had given all he could. He already knew.

Rain swam until he could no longer see the shoreline, until the waters became his sanctuary. And as the rain continued to pour, he realized that sometimes, finding closure doesn't mean forgetting the past. It means accepting it, letting it wash over you like the waves, and finally learning to let go.

When the storm passed, Rain came back to the shore. His body was tired, but his soul felt lighter. He had swum through the storm, not just of the weather, but of his own heart. And for the first time, he felt ready to leave the past behind.

As the sun began to rise, casting a soft light on the water, Olivia stood beside him, her hand resting on his back. They both knew that the storm was over—and that, together, they had found the peace they had both been searching for.

The lesson wasn't in forgetting the past. It was in finding the strength to move forward, knowing that sometimes, letting go is the only way to heal.

The Empty Kennel

Oscar had always been fast. From the first moment he had stepped onto the track, he had known what he was born to do. The wind against his fur, the pounding of his paws against the dirt, the cheering of the crowd—it was his world. For years, he had been one of the fastest greyhounds to race, with a sleek, muscular body built for speed. His coat, dark and glossy, would shine under the lights as he raced past his competitors, his eyes fixed on the finish line. He loved the thrill, the rush of adrenaline, the recognition he received from his owners and fans.

But now, Oscar found himself in an unfamiliar place—a small, quiet kennel on the outskirts of the city, far from the bustling racetrack that had once been his home.

His premature retirement had come suddenly. One moment, he was racing, breaking records and earning accolades, and the next, he was sidelined. A minor injury to his leg had seemed inconsequential at first, but it was enough for the trainers to decide he was no longer fit for the track. The decision had been swift, and with it came the certainty that his racing days were over.

Oscar had never thought about life beyond the track. He had been trained for one purpose—to race—and everything had revolved around that. The days following his retirement were filled with confusion and uncertainty. The once familiar sights and sounds of the track—his teammates, the preparation, the roar of the crowd—were all gone. In their place was an empty kennel, a small space where he was fed and kept, but not needed. He was no longer a champion; he was just another retired dog, waiting for the next chapter that he couldn't yet understand.

At first, he didn't know what to do. His body still felt the energy, the drive, the need to run. But when he ran in the fields behind the kennel, it was different. There was no finish line, no cheering crowd, no sense of purpose. He ran because he had to, because his legs still longed for the freedom of speed, but it didn't feel the same. He didn't know how to find meaning in the stillness of the world outside the track.

He spent his days pacing the kennel, watching the other dogs that had also been retired. Some of them had found a new rhythm—small walks with their owners, lying in the sun, playing with toys. But Oscar couldn't bring himself to do that. He didn't know how to be just a dog, not anymore. His identity had been tied to the races, the glory of being first. Without that, he was unsure who he was.

One evening, as the golden light of the setting sun cast a warm glow over the kennel, a young woman appeared at the gate. She was holding a leash and had a soft smile on her face. Oscar's ears perked up as she approached, her movements calm and inviting. She was an unfamiliar face, but there was something about her energy that made him pause.

"Hey, Oscar," she said gently, reading the tag on his collar. "Ready for a walk?"

Oscar tilted his head, unsure of what to make of this. Walks had never been part of his routine before. It had always been about the track, the speed, the competition. But something about the woman's presence felt different—there was no pressure, no expectation. Just an invitation.

Slowly, he took a few steps forward, and the woman opened the gate, leading him out. They walked through the quiet neighborhood, the sun dipping lower in the sky. The pace was slow, peaceful, nothing like the frantic runs he used to do. As they walked, Oscar felt a sense of calm begin to settle in. He wasn't chasing anything. There was no finish line, no race to win. He could simply walk beside her, taking in the world at his own pace.

Over the weeks that followed, the woman—her name was Emma—continued to take Oscar for daily walks. She didn't push him to run, didn't expect him to perform. She simply let him explore, let him find his own rhythm. At first, Oscar resisted. He would try to pull ahead, eager to break into a sprint, but Emma would gently pull him back, guiding him in a slower, more measured pace.

It wasn't the same as the track. There was no excitement, no glory, no crowd. But gradually, Oscar began to understand something he hadn't before. The joy wasn't in the speed, the records, or the praise. The joy was in the connection, in the simple act of being together—just him and Emma. It was in the quiet walks, the companionship, the peace of the world around them.

Oscar started to relax. He would stop and sniff the air, his tail wagging as he took in the new scents of the world. The need to race began to fade, replaced by a sense of contentment. He no longer defined himself by the track or the victories he had once known. He began to understand that there was more to life than being first.

One day, as Oscar and Emma walked through a park, Emma paused and knelt down beside him. She gently placed her hands on his shoulders, looking into his eyes. "You've done so much, Oscar," she said, her voice soft but filled with admiration. "You've been a champion. But you're more than that. You've shown me that even in retirement, you can still be wonderful. You don't have to be fast to be important. You've taught me that."

Oscar sat there, his head tilted slightly, as if understanding her words. He was no longer the racing dog, the one who lived for the thrill of the track. He was simply Oscar—a dog who had loved to run, who had been a champion in his own right, but who now knew that there was more to life than winning. He had found a new purpose, one that didn't require speed or glory, but simply companionship and love.

As the seasons passed, Oscar and Emma continued their walks, slow and steady, through the quiet streets. Oscar had found his peace, and in doing so, he had learned something that no race could have taught him—that sometimes, the greatest victories are found not in the finish line, but in the journey itself.

Beneath the Willow

Willow had always been proud of her work. As a hunting dog, her days were spent in the fields with her handler, Jake, a rugged man who had raised her from a pup. Together, they had spent countless hours hunting, running through the tall grasses, the scent of pheasants and ducks always in the air. She loved the rhythm of it—the way Jake's voice would guide her, the way her sharp senses could pick up on the slightest rustle in the bushes. It was a bond, a partnership, and for Willow, it was everything.

But that was before the accident.

It had happened one cold autumn morning, the kind of morning where the mist clung to the ground and the world felt silent, except for the sounds of nature waking up. Willow and Jake had set out early, just before dawn, walking into the fields like they had done so many times before. The air was crisp, the ground still damp from the previous night's rain. They moved through the tall grass, Willow leading the way, her nose to the ground, her body tense with focus. It was a perfect morning for a hunt.

But when they reached the edge of the forest, Jake had slipped. One moment he was standing, and the next, he had fallen hard, his foot catching on a rock. The sound of his scream echoed through the trees, a sharp cry that made Willow freeze in her tracks. She rushed back to him, her heart pounding, but it was too late. Jake had injured his leg badly, so badly that he couldn't walk. The pain was evident in his eyes as he tried to push himself up, but his leg wouldn't cooperate. Willow, frantic and unsure of what to do, stayed by his side, nuzzling him gently.

The hours that followed were a blur. Jake was taken to the hospital, and Willow was left behind, waiting in the yard, her tail tucked between her legs. When Jake returned, his leg in a cast, it wasn't just the injury that changed everything—it was the fact that his hunting days were over. The doctors had told him it would take months to recover, but even then, he would never be able to hunt like he once had.

Willow sensed the change immediately. Jake's movements were slower, more careful. He no longer took her out for hunts in the early mornings. The fields were abandoned, and the backyard, once a place of play and work, felt empty. Willow didn't understand why her days had changed so suddenly. Her world had always been defined by the hunt, by the closeness she shared with Jake. But now, he spent most of his days indoors, his gaze often distant, his movements hesitant.

Jake tried to adapt, but the frustration was clear. He could no longer do the thing that had brought him joy, the thing that had kept him connected to Willow. His spirit had dimmed, and though he tried to comfort her with the occasional pat on the head, Willow could tell he wasn't the same. And neither was she.

Months passed, and eventually, the house grew quieter. Willow still waited for the mornings when Jake would take her out, when they could return to their old routines. But they never came. Instead, Willow spent her days lying on the porch, watching the wind sway the trees. Her sense of purpose seemed lost, and the once vibrant dog felt hollow, her energy slowly draining away.

One day, when the weather turned warmer, Jake took Willow for a walk to the old willow tree at the edge of the property, the place where they had often sat together after a long day of hunting. The tree had been a place of solace for them both, the wide branches offering shade and a sense of peace. Jake leaned against the trunk, looking up at the tree's weeping limbs. Willow sat beside him, her head resting against his knee.

"I don't know how to fix this, girl," Jake murmured, his voice thick with frustration. "I used to be able to run, to work with you. But now, it's all different."

Willow looked up at him, her eyes soft with understanding, though she didn't have the words to tell him that she, too, missed the hunts. She missed the partnership, the adventure, and the companionship. She wanted to help him, wanted to give him back what had been taken from him. But she didn't know how.

As they sat there, a car pulled into the driveway, and Jake straightened up. A family stepped out—another couple with two children. The man, Thomas, was carrying a large crate, and the woman, Marissa, was holding the hand of a young girl who had a pained look in her eyes. It took a moment for Willow to realize what was happening, but when she did, something shifted within her.

The family approached, and Thomas looked at Jake with a gentle smile. "We've heard a lot about you and your dog," he said. "We were wondering if you'd be willing to help us."

Jake glanced at Willow, confusion crossing his face. "Help? How?"

Marissa stepped forward, her voice quiet. "Our daughter, Lily... she's been struggling with something. Grief, really. We lost our old dog a few months ago. And Lily's been withdrawn since then, barely speaking. We've tried everything, but nothing seems to reach her."

Willow's ears perked up at the mention of grief. She understood grief. She had been grieving the loss of the old rhythm of her life, of the hunts, of the days spent running through the fields with Jake. Lily's grief was different, but perhaps, in some way, it was the same. Willow stood up, her legs stiff but determined, and walked toward the young girl.

Lily looked at Willow with wide, unsure eyes. The girl had been quiet throughout the conversation, but now, she knelt down, slowly reaching out a hand. Willow, with a softness that had returned to her heart, sat down beside the girl and nuzzled her gently. The girl hesitated for a moment, then allowed herself to pet Willow's fur.

For the first time in a long time, Willow felt a spark of purpose. She didn't need to race or hunt to make a difference. She could still help, still offer the same companionship that had once meant so much to Jake. Willow stayed close to Lily, her presence offering a quiet comfort, a non-verbal understanding that she, too, had experienced loss.

Over time, Lily began to open up. She would sit with Willow in the backyard, talking to her as if she could understand every word. Slowly, the girl's grief began to ease, her laughter returning in small, hesitant bursts. Willow continued to be there, her steady presence offering a sense of peace that words couldn't.

One evening, as the sun dipped low behind the willow tree, Jake watched Willow and Lily sitting together, the bond between them growing stronger each day. And for the first time since his injury, Jake realized something. Willow had found a new purpose. She had become the source of healing—not just for him, but for someone else who needed her.

In the end, Willow didn't need to return to the hunt to be whole. She had found her place once again, not through speed or strength, but through the quiet comfort of her companionship and the bond she shared with those she loved. And as the wind whispered through the branches of the willow tree, she knew that even after loss, there was still a way forward.

Shadows of the Night

Midnight had always been a dog of the night. His glossy black coat blended perfectly with the shadows, his eyes sharp and watchful as he stood guard at the front door, waiting for anything out of place. He had been trained as a guard dog from the moment he was a puppy. His owner, George, had always trusted him completely. They made a perfect team—George with his calm demeanor and steady hands, and Midnight with his loyalty and sharp instincts. Together, they had lived in the same house for years, their routine as predictable as the rising and setting of the sun.

But now, it was just Midnight.

The house was quiet, the air heavy with the weight of absence. The sounds that used to fill the rooms—George's laughter, the tapping of his boots as he walked through the hall, the rustling of his jacket—were gone. Midnight missed them, but there was something more profound he felt now, something he couldn't name. It was a hollow emptiness that stretched through the entire house. The once lively place, filled with purpose, now seemed like a mausoleum, a place that belonged to no one.

George had passed away suddenly, a heart attack that took him in the middle of the night. Midnight had been there, lying at his feet as he always did, when the life drained from his body. The vet had come and confirmed it, but Midnight already knew. He had felt it in the air, sensed the change in George's steady breathing. And now, he was left alone to protect the house, to keep watch as he had always done. But this time, there was no one to watch over.

The first few days after George's death were filled with confusion. Midnight paced the house, waiting for George to return, but the hours turned into days, and George never came. Midnight's instincts told him to stay, to guard the house as he had always done, but each passing day made the emptiness more pronounced. His watch over the house became more routine, more mechanical, but the presence of the man he loved was gone.

Nightfall became his hardest time. George had always been there with him during the long nights, watching the moon rise through the windows, keeping each other company through the quiet hours. But now, Midnight stood alone in the darkness, his body tense as he listened for sounds that no longer came. The house creaked in the wind, the branches of trees scratched against the windows, but no footsteps echoed through the halls. Midnight would sit by the door, eyes locked on the shadows outside, waiting for a threat that would never come.

One evening, as the moon rose high in the sky, Midnight stood by the window, his eyes scanning the yard. The darkness stretched out before him, deep and endless, but tonight, there was something different. He could hear a sound, something soft but persistent—a faint rustling in the bushes near the garden wall. Midnight's ears perked up, his body tensing in anticipation. His instincts kicked in, and he slowly moved to the door, paws silent on the hardwood floor.

He opened the door cautiously, his eyes narrowing as he peered into the night. The rustling continued, and Midnight's muscles coiled, ready to spring into action. But as he stepped outside, a chill ran through him. There was no immediate danger, no intruder lurking in the shadows. The noise was just the wind brushing through the leaves. But for some reason, tonight, the wind felt different—heavier, colder, as if it carried the weight of his own fears.

Midnight stood in the yard, staring at the empty space where George had once worked, where they had spent countless evenings together. The yard was still, the trees unmoving, and yet, the silence around him felt louder than ever. The moon cast long shadows across the ground, and for a moment, Midnight felt as if he were standing on the edge of an abyss, a place where the darkness never ended.

He stayed outside longer than usual, standing vigil in the night. He could hear the sound of his own breathing, could feel his heartbeat echoing in his chest. The loneliness weighed down on him like a physical presence, pulling at him, threatening to crush him. Midnight longed for the familiar presence of George, for the comfort of knowing someone was there with him. But as the hours passed, the fear began to subside. Midnight realized that George would never come back. The man who had loved him, who had cared for him, was gone. And yet, he remained.

As dawn approached, Midnight finally turned and made his way back into the house. He walked slowly, his paws heavy with exhaustion. He stood at the doorway, looking back one last time at the yard where they had once spent so many nights together. The silence of the house greeted him, the familiar creaks of the old wooden floors echoing in the emptiness.

But then, something shifted within him. Midnight lay down in his usual spot by the door, his head resting on his paws. The shadows in the house no longer seemed as oppressive. The house was empty, yes, but it was also his home. And though George was no longer there, Midnight still had a purpose—to protect, to guard, to honor the memory of the man who had trusted him.

The darkness of the night no longer held the same fear. Midnight realized that his watch didn't have to end with George's passing. The fear of being alone, of standing in the shadows, was still there, but it no longer defined him. He could stand guard, not just for George, but for the home they had shared. The love that had once filled the house hadn't disappeared. It was still with him, woven into every part of the walls, the floor, the yard. And perhaps, in time, he would learn to accept the silence, to stand watch with the same devotion he had always known.

As the sun began to rise, casting a soft light over the room, Midnight closed his eyes. He was alone, yes. But he was also strong, still holding onto the memories of a time when the house had been full of life. The shadows no longer scared him, for he had learned that sometimes, the greatest strength is found in standing firm, even when the darkness seems endless.

And as the light of the new day filtered through the window, Midnight knew that though George was gone, the love they had shared would remain, a silent bond that could never be broken.

Fading Paws

Penny had always been a dog of energy and purpose. As a young puppy, she had bounded across the fields with the kind of enthusiasm only a dog can possess, her ears flapping in the wind, her tail a blur behind her. She had been the one to chase after sticks, the one to run alongside the children as they rode their bikes, the one to curl up by the fire at night with her family. For years, Penny had been at the heart of everything—a loyal companion, a protector, and a friend.

Now, at the age of fourteen, Penny's legs had grown stiff. The joy of chasing after the ball had become a distant memory, replaced by slow, labored walks and long naps in the sun. The once-vibrant fur that had adorned her body had grayed, especially around her muzzle, and her once-sharp eyes had dulled, though the love she felt for her family remained unchanged. Time had taken its toll, and Penny could feel it in every movement, in every creak of her joints, in every breath that came just a little slower than it used to.

She spent most of her days lying by the window, watching the world go by. She no longer had the energy to join the children in their games, and the house had become quieter, the once-chaotic noise of their laughter replaced with a more peaceful, gentler atmosphere. The family had grown older, too—two of the children had moved out, and the youngest had started spending more time with friends, leaving Penny alone with her humans, who were now older and quieter as well.

Penny often reflected on the generations she had watched over. She had been there when the children were born, when they took their first steps, when they learned how to ride their bikes and when they left for their first day of school. She had been there for their triumphs and their heartbreaks, a silent witness to the passage of time.

Her memory wandered back to the first day she had arrived at the family's home as a puppy. She had been so small then, so full of life. The children had squealed in delight when they saw her, and she had been surrounded by laughter and excitement. Those early years had been full of energy—family outings, trips to the park, and endless hours of play. Penny had always been in the thick of it, her heart full of joy at the simple act of being with her family.

As the years passed, her role changed, but she had never minded. She had watched the children grow, and as they aged, she had aged with them. She had become their comfort, their constant, always there for them when the world felt too big or too hard. And as they grew into adulthood, she had silently stood guard over them, offering her quiet, unspoken support. Penny had never asked for much—just to be by their side, to watch over them, to share in the quiet moments.

But now, as she lay in her favorite spot by the window, Penny couldn't help but wonder how much time she had left. The aches in her body were becoming harder to ignore, and the weight of her age pressed down on her in a way it never had before. She had seen so much, had loved so fiercely, but the days of chasing after sticks and running through the fields were behind her. She had fulfilled her purpose, but the thought of leaving—of no longer being there for her family—was a thought she could not yet fully accept.

One evening, as the sun began to set, casting a soft golden light over the house, Penny's family gathered in the living room. The children, now adults, were sitting on the couch, talking softly among themselves. Penny lay at their feet, watching them with a sense of contentment. The youngest child, Emma, reached down and gently scratched behind Penny's ears.

"You're getting old, girl," Emma said softly, her voice tinged with sadness. Penny's tail gave a weak thump against the floor, but she didn't move. She had known for a while that the family could see her aging, could feel the slow passing of time.

Penny had never been one to resist change. She had always known that life was a series of moments, each one leading to the next, and that even the best moments couldn't last forever. She had accepted the changes in her family, had witnessed their growth and their losses, and had always been there for them, a constant in the ebb and flow of life. But now, she faced a change of her own—a change that would take her from the only life she had ever known.

As the evening drew on and the last of the light faded from the sky, Penny's family quietly gathered around her. They knew. They had seen the signs—the slowing steps, the quiet moments of stillness—and though no one spoke of it aloud, they all knew that it was time.

Emma bent down and whispered to Penny, "You've been the best dog, the best companion we could have ever asked for. Thank you, for everything."

Penny's tail gave one last slow thump against the floor, and in that moment, she understood. She had given her love, her loyalty, her everything to her family, and they had given her the same in return. It wasn't the end of the road, Penny realized, but simply the next step in the journey. She didn't need to fear it, because she knew that the love she had shared with them would never be gone. It would live on in their hearts, just as it would live on in hers.

With a final, contented sigh, Penny closed her eyes. She had watched over her family for so many years, and now it was time for her to rest. She would never be forgotten.

The house, quiet and still, felt like home—the home she had built through the years of unconditional love. And as she faded into sleep, Penny understood that sometimes the greatest gift a dog can give is not just love, but the ability to let go, knowing that the bonds we share will continue to guide us even when we can no longer walk beside the ones we love.

In the stillness, as the family whispered their goodbyes, Penny's presence lingered—unseen, but never forgotten.

The Last Ride

Rex had always been a dog of purpose. From the moment he was a pup, he had been trained for one mission—to help others. His gentle nature, steady gaze, and unwavering loyalty made him the perfect therapy dog. He worked at the local hospital, visiting patients who needed comfort, children who needed reassurance, and elderly folks who just wanted someone to listen without judgment. He had been a lifeline for so many, but there was one person in particular who needed him more than anyone else—Elliott.

Elliott was only eight years old when his mother, Sarah, was diagnosed with cancer. The news hit their family like a storm. Sarah had been the rock of their small family, and Elliott had always been close to her, spending his days playing in the backyard and drawing pictures with her by his side. But as Sarah's illness progressed, things began to change. The hospital visits became frequent, and Sarah's once vibrant energy slowly drained away. Elliott had a hard time understanding what was happening—why his mother was always tired, why she had to go to the hospital so often, why she couldn't play with him the way she used to. And as the months went on, it became clear that the illness was winning.

Through it all, Rex had been there. He had arrived at Sarah and Elliott's home when Sarah's illness first started to weigh on them, as a companion for both mother and son. While Sarah tried to find comfort in her treatment, it was Rex who stayed by Elliott's side during the long nights when the fear of losing his mother would grip him. He would curl up next to the boy, his head resting on Elliott's lap, offering quiet comfort. Rex understood more than most. He could sense the emotions, feel the sadness and the anxiety, and he always knew how to be just what Elliott needed—whether that was a soft nudge, a lick on the hand, or simply sitting there silently with him.

As Sarah's health continued to decline, the moments of joy grew fewer. Elliott would spend hours sitting with his mother, holding her hand, talking to her as she slept, and Rex would lay beside them, keeping watch. Even when Sarah's strength failed her, Rex's presence was constant. It was the simple act of being there that mattered most, not the words.

One evening, as autumn began to settle in and the leaves outside turned golden and red, Sarah's condition worsened. She had spent the day sleeping, barely able to lift her head. Elliott sat beside her, clutching Rex's leash in one hand and holding his mother's hand in the other. There was a stillness in the room, a quiet tension that seemed to hang in the air.

"Rex," Elliott whispered, looking at his mother's pale face, "will she be okay?"

Rex raised his head and looked at Elliott with his steady, brown eyes. He could feel the weight of the question, and though he couldn't answer in words, he nudged Elliott's hand, letting the boy know he wasn't alone. There was no way to make the pain disappear, no magic word to take away the fear, but Rex would stay by Elliott's side. He always had.

The days passed slowly, and Sarah's condition became more frail. She was no longer able to sit up, no longer able to speak, but Elliott stayed with her, never leaving her side, always holding her hand. Rex never strayed far from them, offering the kind of comfort only a dog could provide—a calm, steady presence in the face of uncertainty.

The day came when Sarah's breathing slowed, and the familiar rise and fall of her chest became less and less noticeable. It was in the quiet hours of the morning, the house still and empty of sound, that Sarah's heart finally stopped. She had fought, she had held on, but the illness had taken everything from her.

Elliott sat by her side, his head in his hands, tears streaming down his face. Rex, ever loyal, sat beside him, his body close to Elliott's, offering the kind of silent support that could never be fully understood in words.

For a long time, Elliott didn't move. He didn't know how to. The world had changed, and in that moment, he felt as if it had collapsed around him. His mother was gone, and there was nothing left but the emptiness of the house, the absence of her presence.

And yet, in the quiet that followed, Rex did something Elliott didn't expect. He nudged Elliott gently, and then stood, walking to the front door. He turned back to Elliott, giving him one last, hopeful look, as if to say, *it's time.*

Elliott wiped his eyes and stood slowly, following Rex as the dog led him outside. They walked into the backyard, where the morning sun had just begun to rise, casting a soft glow over the earth. Rex led Elliott to the old oak tree in the corner of the yard, the same place where Sarah used to sit with him, and where she and Elliott had spent hours playing together in happier times.

There, under the shade of the tree, Rex stopped. He sat down, looking up at Elliott with calm, knowing eyes. And for the first time in days, Elliott felt something shift inside him. He didn't know how to let go of his mother, how to move on from the pain of losing her, but standing there beside Rex—his faithful companion—Elliott realized something. His grief was part of him, a part that would always remain. But there was still life to live, still moments to embrace, even in the wake of loss.

Rex remained by his side, and Elliott sat down next to him, leaning his head on the dog's soft fur. Together, they sat in silence, the bond between them unspoken, but clear. Elliott wasn't alone. He had Rex, and Rex had always understood him, understood the quiet moments, the unspoken pain, the weight of loss. Together, they would face the days ahead, one step at a time.

And in that quiet morning light, amidst the pain, Elliott realized that healing didn't mean forgetting. It meant moving forward, slowly but surely, with the support of those who had been with him all along. Even if words could never express it, love was there—quiet, constant, and unwavering, like the bond he shared with Rex.

And as Rex rested his head against Elliott's knee, they sat together beneath the oak tree, ready for the next step in the journey.

Autumn Leaves

Maple had always loved the fall. The crisp air, the smell of damp earth and pine, and the vibrant colors of the leaves as they fluttered down from the trees—these were the moments she lived for. As a young, energetic dog, she had always felt a rush of joy when autumn came. The air seemed to invite her into the world outside, and she would race through the yard, chasing after the leaves that danced and swirled in the wind. Her owner, Eleanor, would laugh and cheer her on, tossing the leaves into the air just to see Maple leap and twist to catch them. They shared a special bond, one built on simple moments like these.

For years, they had spent every autumn together, creating a ritual of sorts. Maple would run through the yard, her paws kicking up leaves, while Eleanor sat on the porch, smiling as she watched. It was their tradition, something that made the cool autumn mornings feel warm, and the long afternoons feel endless in the best way possible. The sound of the wind rustling through the trees, the occasional call of a bird overhead—it was their world, a world where nothing seemed to change.

But this autumn was different.

Eleanor had grown quieter over the last few months. Maple could sense it, though she didn't fully understand why. The walks had become shorter, and the moments of joy Maple had once shared with Eleanor felt fewer. Instead, Maple often found her owner sitting in a chair by the window, staring out at the yard, lost in thought. The sparkle in Eleanor's eyes that Maple had always known seemed dimmer now, replaced by a kind of weariness that never quite left.

One afternoon, Eleanor sat on the porch, and Maple, as usual, bounded toward her, wagging her tail and ready for their game. But this time, Eleanor didn't stand up, didn't even look up when Maple approached. She simply reached out, gently petting Maple's head. Her hand felt slower, weaker than it had before.

"We won't be playing much this autumn, my dear," Eleanor said softly, almost to herself. Maple tilted her head, unsure of what she meant.

It wasn't until a few days later that Eleanor explained what she had meant. A doctor had visited the house, and Eleanor had been diagnosed with a condition that would make it difficult for her to care for herself. The doctor spoke kindly, gently suggesting that it would be best for Eleanor to move to a care facility where she could receive proper attention. Eleanor was reluctant, but Maple saw the sadness in her eyes. Eleanor wasn't the same.

The following weeks were full of packing, of strangers in and out of the house, and of quieter moments between the two of them. Maple tried to stay close, as if she could will Eleanor to stay. But on the day Eleanor left for the care facility, Maple watched her owner climb into the back of a car, her face pressed against the glass, a soft goodbye whispered as the car pulled away.

Maple stayed in the house, waiting for Eleanor to come back. She kept to her usual spot on the porch, her eyes fixed on the driveway, hoping to see Eleanor return. But days passed, then weeks, and no one came.

Without Eleanor, the yard felt empty, the once-vibrant autumn leaves now just a reminder of the times they had shared. Maple couldn't understand why the world felt so different now. She wandered through the yard, but the joy of chasing the leaves was gone. She had always been so full of life when Eleanor was with her. But now, there was a hollow emptiness in her chest that nothing seemed to fill.

As the autumn days stretched on, Maple found herself growing more and more despondent. She no longer ran after the leaves, no longer chased them through the yard. Instead, she would sit by the fence, her tail still but her gaze lost in the distance. The world had shifted, and she wasn't sure where she fit anymore.

But then, something unexpected happened.

One afternoon, a little boy from the neighborhood appeared at the gate. He was holding a small, brightly colored leaf in his hand, his face lit up with curiosity. Maple had seen him around before, but this time, he seemed to notice her in a way he hadn't before.

"Hey there," the boy said softly, as if unsure how to approach her. "I saw you and the lady chase leaves together before. You like that too, huh?" He gently tossed the leaf into the air, and it fluttered down toward Maple. The dog stood up and sniffed at the leaf, her ears perked, and for a moment, something stirred in her.

The boy watched her with a shy smile, and Maple, in a hesitant but instinctive motion, began to nudge the leaf with her nose, sending it spinning in the wind. The boy giggled and clapped his hands. "That's it! You can still chase them! Let's play together!"

And so, for the first time in what felt like forever, Maple ran. She chased the leaf, her legs moving faster than she had in weeks, her tail wagging again, her eyes bright with the joy of the game. The boy cheered her on, and Maple realized something she hadn't thought about before. The world hadn't completely changed. There were still moments to enjoy, still small joys to be found, even in the quiet of her new life. She might not have Eleanor with her right now, but she could still find happiness in the little things.

Over the following weeks, the boy visited regularly, sometimes with leaves in hand, other times just sitting by the fence, talking to Maple like an old friend. And though Maple missed Eleanor deeply, she began to understand that change didn't always mean loss. Sometimes, it meant finding new paths, new connections, and new ways to enjoy the world.

One crisp evening, as the last of the autumn leaves fluttered to the ground, Maple stood in the yard, the wind brushing through her fur. She watched the golden leaves swirl around her feet, and for a moment, she could almost hear Eleanor's laugh, as if the old days hadn't gone at all. The boy appeared, as he always did, and together, they watched the leaves fall together, Maple's heart swelling in a way it hadn't in a long time.

The autumn leaves would always remind her of the past, of the days spent running with Eleanor. But they also reminded her that life continued, that there was always room for new beginnings—even in the smallest, most unexpected ways.

Silent Companion

Buddy had never known the world in the way most dogs did. From the moment he was born, his eyes had been clouded, unable to perceive the world around him in vivid colors or sharp details. But Buddy didn't mind—he had learned to navigate the world through his other senses: the soft rustle of leaves in the breeze, the scent of food from the kitchen, the warmth of his owner's hand resting gently on his back.

His owner, Sarah, had taken him in as a puppy. She had been patient with him, showing him the world with kindness and love. Sarah was elderly, and over the years, her own health had started to decline, her steps slowing, her body aching. But Buddy had always been her constant companion, the one who knew her rhythms, her habits, her needs.

In the early days, when Sarah's vision had started to fade and she had begun to need more assistance, Buddy had naturally stepped into the role of her guide. He would sit by her side as she walked through the house, his sensitive ears trained to pick up any potential obstacles, gently nudging her to the left or right if she needed direction. When she dropped something, Buddy was there, nudging it back into her hand with his nose. At the grocery store, Sarah would hold his harness, and he would lead her down the aisles, guiding her safely through the crowd.

Buddy's world had been a quiet one, filled with familiar sounds and smells, and Sarah's presence had always been the center of it. As Sarah's health began to worsen, Buddy noticed the changes. Her breath had become more labored, her movements slower, and the once-vibrant energy she had always carried with her seemed to fade. Yet, Buddy remained as constant as ever, always by her side, always ready to help however he could.

But as Sarah's condition grew more serious, the once simple tasks became more difficult. She had fallen a few times, her balance unsteady, and the fear of something worse happening loomed. Buddy could feel the tension in the air as Sarah moved more cautiously around the house. It wasn't just her body that was frail—it was her spirit, too. She had always been independent, but now, she found herself needing Buddy in ways she hadn't before.

One evening, after Sarah had finished her dinner, she moved slowly to the living room chair. Buddy followed her, his paws soft on the floor, and sat beside her, his head resting on her knee as she reached down to pat him.

"I don't know how much longer I can do this, Buddy," Sarah whispered, her voice weak, her hand trembling slightly as it ran over his fur. "You've been such a good boy, but I'm getting tired. I don't want to be a burden."

Buddy nuzzled her hand, sensing the sorrow in her words, and though he couldn't see her tears, he could feel the tremble of her fingers, the weight of her unspoken fears. He had always known her, every part of her, but now, with her health declining, it was as if both of them were facing a future they weren't prepared for. Buddy had always relied on his other senses, but now, as his own body aged, his fears began to creep in. The uncertainty of what would happen if Sarah couldn't care for herself any longer made him anxious. What would he do without her?

The days grew quieter. Sarah's health continued to decline, and the light in her eyes seemed to dim with each passing day. Buddy had become even more vigilant, following her wherever she went, guiding her as she slowly moved from room to room. At night, he would curl up beside her bed, his body stretched out in an attempt to protect her from the darkness he couldn't see but could still feel pressing in on them.

One morning, Sarah didn't wake up right away. Buddy nudged her gently, licking her hand, trying to wake her, but she didn't stir. His heart began to race. He had never felt so helpless. He barked once, then twice, but there was no response. Panic began to rise in his chest as he paced beside her bed, unsure of what to do. He couldn't understand why she didn't get up like she usually did.

It wasn't until Sarah's caretaker arrived that the situation was understood. Sarah had passed away in her sleep, her body finally giving in to the illness that had taken over. The loss was not sudden, but it was still a shock. Buddy stood by her side, his tail low, his eyes filled with confusion and sorrow. She was gone, and for the first time in his life, Buddy didn't know what to do next. The world that had once been so full of routine, of purpose, now felt foreign, empty.

In the days that followed, Buddy was moved into a new home. He was adopted by a family that lived nearby, kind people who had heard about his bond with Sarah. They understood that Buddy had lived a life of deep attachment, and they made sure to be gentle with him. There were two children in the house, a boy and a girl, both eager to welcome Buddy into their lives.

At first, Buddy resisted. He would lie in the corner, his head down, unsure of his place in this new environment. He missed Sarah—her familiar scent, her soft voice, the way she used to hold him close. But little by little, the children began to show him love and care. They fed him, took him on walks, and spoke to him in gentle tones. They even let him sit beside them during the evenings, watching TV together. Buddy still felt the absence of Sarah, but he began to understand that not all bonds were meant to be broken.

One afternoon, after the children had taken him to the park, Buddy found himself standing beneath a large tree. The autumn leaves were falling around him, the crisp air filling his nose with new smells. He stood still for a moment, listening to the soft rustling of the leaves. It reminded him of the days with Sarah, of the mornings they had spent together, the way she would sit on the porch and watch the leaves fall.

Buddy closed his eyes for a moment, remembering those days. And then, he felt something—something in the air that made him stand taller. The sun was setting, the golden light casting long shadows across the ground, and for the first time since Sarah's passing, Buddy felt at peace. He couldn't replace her, nor could he forget her, but he had found a new rhythm. He had learned to adapt, to let love in again, even in the face of loss.

He turned back toward the family, his tail wagging softly, and walked toward them with a newfound calm. There was still so much he couldn't see, but there was so much he could feel. And in that moment, Buddy understood that life—though filled with loss—also held room for new beginnings.

The Lone Howl

Luna had always been the center of the family's world. From the moment she was brought home as a puppy, she had been surrounded by laughter and love. She would follow her humans everywhere, her tail wagging furiously, excited to share every moment with them. The family—Maggie, Tim, and their two children—had showered Luna with attention. She had her own cozy bed by the fireplace, her leash always ready for their walks in the park, and she was the first to cuddle up next to them at the end of each long day.

Luna had never imagined that anything would change. She was their girl, their constant companion. But when a new addition arrived—a small, excitable golden retriever puppy named Max—Luna's world began to shift.

It started subtly. First, there were the extra trips to the pet store, the excited whispers, the new bed placed next to hers, and the soft cooing sounds as they brought Max into the house. Luna had always been the one who greeted Maggie and Tim at the door with excited jumps, but now, Max was there, jumping higher, wagging more, taking up more space.

At first, Luna had tried to be kind. She allowed Max to explore the house, gave him the occasional sniff, but it didn't take long before she felt the change. Max wasn't just a new puppy; he was a new center of attention. Every walk was about Max learning to heel, every treat was given to Max first. Luna would watch from the corner, her ears drooping, her tail low. She had never known what jealousy was, but she felt it now—this new puppy was taking something she had always had.

As days passed, Luna became more withdrawn. The walks that had once been filled with laughter and excitement now felt like a chore. She would lag behind, keeping her distance as Max bounded ahead, the sound of his tiny paws racing through the grass always a little too loud in her ears. When they were indoors, Luna would retreat to her bed, watching as the family gathered around Max, cooing over his cuteness, playing with him in ways they had once played with her.

The nights were the hardest. Luna had always slept at the foot of Maggie's bed, a safe and warm place. But now, Max was there, too. The little puppy had claimed the space beside Maggie's pillow, and Luna was left to curl up in the corner. The warmth of the bed, once shared with love, now felt empty.

One evening, as the family settled down on the couch, Luna watched them all, her paws folded beneath her, the quiet loneliness growing heavier in her chest. Max was asleep in Tim's lap, the children were giggling softly at the puppy's twitching paws, and Maggie stroked Max's golden fur with a loving smile. But Luna couldn't help the bitter sting in her heart. She had given so much of herself to this family, and now, it felt as if she had been replaced.

Unable to bear it any longer, Luna slipped out of the room, her heart heavy with the weight of abandonment. She pushed through the dog door into the backyard, where the evening air felt cool against her fur. The yard was quiet, the night still, but Luna felt the hollowness in her chest, a space that seemed impossible to fill.

She walked through the yard, slowly, head down, her paws dragging in the dirt. It was then that she heard the howl—the soft, mournful sound of a coyote in the distance, calling out into the empty night. Luna's ears perked up, and she paused, her head turning toward the sound. It reminded her of the nights she used to spend under the stars with Maggie, listening to the sounds of the world, feeling like she belonged to something bigger.

Luna's own voice rose in response, her howl echoing into the darkened night. It was a long, lonely sound—one that spoke of her sadness, her confusion, and her desire to be heard. For a moment, Luna felt a strange sense of relief as her voice cut through the quiet of the night. She was still here. She was still alive, still part of this world.

But as the howl faded into the distance, Luna's heart sank. She had tried to make her feelings known, but the emptiness lingered. She walked back to the house, her paws slow and heavy, her mind filled with questions she couldn't answer.

The following weeks were filled with the same routine. Max, the puppy, seemed to thrive in the attention, while Luna became more distant, unsure of her place. She started to spend more time outside, laying in the sun or wandering around the backyard. She didn't bark when the doorbell rang or wag her tail at the children anymore. She simply lay still, watching the world go by, feeling like she was no longer part of it.

It wasn't until one rainy afternoon, when the sky was dark and the air heavy with the scent of earth, that Luna finally understood. She was outside, sitting beneath the old oak tree, when Max came running toward her, his tiny paws splashing in the puddles. He had gotten wet, and his fur was soaked, but his eyes were wide with excitement as he approached her.

"Luna! Luna!" Max barked, his tail wagging furiously. "Come play with me! Come on!"

Luna looked at him, her heart heavy with the pain of the past few weeks. But then, something in Max's eyes softened. He wasn't trying to replace her—he was simply trying to be her friend. And for the first time in a long while, Luna felt the stirrings of something else, something she hadn't realized she missed—connection.

Slowly, Luna rose to her feet and padded toward Max. He jumped in front of her, his tail wagging harder than ever, and he nudged her gently with his nose. With a soft growl of playfulness, Luna took a step forward, and then another, and soon, they were running through the rain-soaked yard together, their paws splashing in the puddles, their laughter ringing out in the air.

The jealousy, the abandonment, the hurt—all of it began to fade away, replaced by the simple joy of companionship. Max wasn't taking her place. He was a new part of the family, a new companion to share in the happiness they had always known. Luna realized, in that moment, that her heart had room for more than just one.

The autumn days passed, and Luna's feelings shifted. She still had her moments of quiet longing, but she had learned to accept the changes in her family. Max had a place, and so did she. The love they shared was bigger than just one person, bigger than just one dog. There was enough room for both of them.

And as the seasons continued to change, Luna learned that sometimes, letting go of the past and embracing the new didn't mean losing what you had—it meant making space for something even better.

Garden of Memories

Daisy had always been gentle, her golden coat soft against the sunlight that filtered through the trees in the hospice garden. She had been a therapy dog for the last five years, her role clear and her mission simple: bring comfort to those whose time was running out. The hospice garden, with its winding paths and blooming flowers, was her domain. She had come to know every corner of it—the sweet fragrance of the roses, the quiet rustle of the leaves in the wind, the soft murmur of the fountain. Each day, she would walk alongside the patients, her eyes full of understanding as they shared their stories, their sorrows, and their fears.

There was something calming about Daisy, something steady in the way she would sit beside them, her head gently resting on their laps or her nose nudging their hands. For some, it was the soft warmth of her presence that made the unbearable seem a little easier. For others, it was the quiet companionship, the way Daisy listened with her heart, never needing words. She had seen many people come and go, each person different, each leaving their mark on her heart. But among the faces and names, one person stood out—Mrs. Emerson.

Mrs. Emerson was one of the first patients Daisy had met at the hospice. A sharp, dignified woman in her late seventies, Mrs. Emerson had a quiet but determined strength. She had been suffering from cancer, her body slowly succumbing to the illness, but her mind was as sharp as ever. Daisy was drawn to her from the first moment they met. Mrs. Emerson would sit in her favorite spot by the rose garden, her fingers delicately stroking Daisy's coat as they sat together in silence.

"Do you miss him too?" Mrs. Emerson had asked Daisy one day, her voice soft as she gazed out at the flowers. Daisy's ears perked up, but she didn't answer. Of course, she missed him too—she had learned to read the sadness in her owner's eyes. The man Mrs. Emerson spoke of, her husband, had passed away many years ago, but the sorrow had never truly left her. Daisy, ever the gentle listener, would nuzzle her, offering her quiet comfort without words.

Over time, Daisy's bond with Mrs. Emerson deepened. Every day, she would visit, her tail wagging as she trotted over to the elderly woman. And each time, Mrs. Emerson would smile, her face softening with the warmth Daisy brought. The days were marked by their shared moments in the garden—whether it was a quiet walk along the stone paths or sitting together in the late afternoon sunlight. Mrs. Emerson often told Daisy stories of her late husband, of the life they had built together, of the love they had shared.

But one morning, Daisy sensed a change. The air was cooler, and Mrs. Emerson had grown quieter. She was no longer sitting outside in the garden as often, and when she did, she looked tired. Her once-vibrant eyes were now clouded with exhaustion, and Daisy could feel the difference in her touch. Mrs. Emerson's fingers no longer gently stroked Daisy's fur with the same strength—they were lighter, slower. Daisy sat at her feet, resting her head on Mrs. Emerson's lap as she had so many times before, but this time, there was an unspoken sense of finality in the air. It was as if Mrs. Emerson, too, could feel that her time was drawing near.

One afternoon, as the sun dipped low in the sky, casting long shadows over the garden, Daisy found herself by Mrs. Emerson's side once again. The older woman had requested to sit by the rose bushes, where she had always found comfort, and Daisy followed her, sitting patiently beside her. This time, however, Mrs. Emerson didn't speak as she usually did. She simply gazed out at the roses, her face peaceful, yet tinged with sorrow.

"Do you think he's waiting for me?" Mrs. Emerson whispered, her voice barely audible. "I wonder if he's been watching, waiting for me, just like I've waited for him all these years."

Daisy, her eyes full of understanding, nudged her gently with her nose. She didn't need to say anything—she had learned over the years that not all pain needed to be spoken aloud. Some things, like love and loss, were just understood. And in that moment, Daisy understood Mrs. Emerson's grief—the longing that never quite went away, no matter how much time passed.

As the days went by, Mrs. Emerson's condition worsened. She became weaker, spending more time resting in her room rather than enjoying the garden. Daisy continued to visit, her presence always calm, always steadfast. She would curl up beside Mrs. Emerson's bed, offering her company in the quiet hours of the day. And every time, Mrs. Emerson would smile, her wrinkled hand resting on Daisy's fur as she drifted in and out of sleep.

The day Mrs. Emerson passed away, the sky was overcast, a soft drizzle falling over the garden. Daisy lay beside her, her head resting on the bed, her eyes gazing up at the stillness of the room. The moment was quiet, peaceful, as if the earth itself had taken a breath. There was no dramatic finality, no overwhelming sense of loss—it was simply the passing of time, the way it always had been.

In the days that followed, the hospice garden felt emptier than it ever had before. Daisy wandered through the familiar paths, the flowers blooming around her, but she didn't feel the joy she once had in the vibrant colors. She missed Mrs. Emerson. She missed the stories, the gentle words, the companionship.

But then, one morning, something shifted. Daisy found herself standing in the rose garden once again, her paws pressing into the soft earth. The roses had bloomed more brightly than before, their colors vivid against the gray sky. As Daisy sat, she remembered Mrs. Emerson's words about her husband waiting for her. Perhaps, in that moment, Daisy realized something she hadn't before: love wasn't bound by time. It didn't fade away, nor did it vanish with death. It lived on, in memories, in moments shared, in the lives we touch.

Daisy took a deep breath, the soft scent of the roses filling her senses. She had given comfort, as she always had, and perhaps now, she would be ready to offer it again. The hospice garden was her home, and though she had lost a dear friend, she knew that her purpose remained.

With one last look at the blooming roses, Daisy stood up, her tail wagging softly. She walked away, her heart heavy but full of quiet resolve, knowing that love, in all its forms, never truly fades. It endures—through memories, through moments, and through the heartbeats of those who remember. And so, with each step, Daisy found the courage to keep moving forward.

The Last Chase

Scout had always been a dog of boundless energy. From the first moment he had run through the open fields as a young puppy, he had known the thrill of the wind in his fur, the soft earth beneath his paws, and the exhilarating freedom of speed. His family—James, Claire, and their two children, Ben and Lucy—had always known Scout as the dog who never stopped. He would chase after sticks, race the kids through the park, and lead them on endless adventures along the trails behind their house. For Scout, there was nothing better than the feeling of running, the joy of moving through the world at his own pace.

But as the years passed, Scout began to slow. First, it was subtle—his steps weren't as quick, his breath wasn't as steady after a run. Claire noticed it first, watching him lie down more often, his eyes clouded with a kind of weariness. The kids, growing older themselves, began to notice that Scout didn't seem as eager to chase after them in the yard, or to race along the trails they used to run together. James tried to keep their favorite walks through the forest and fields a regular part of their weekend routine, but as time went on, Scout's pace slowed, and the joy he once had seemed to fade.

It wasn't until the vet gave them the news that Claire truly understood how much had changed. Scout had arthritis, and his once-strong legs were giving out. His joints, once fluid and fast, were now stiff and painful. The vet spoke in soft, careful tones, offering medication and suggestions, but it was clear that time was catching up with Scout. The dog who had spent his life running was now facing a future where running would be nothing but a memory.

One evening, as the sun set low behind the trees and the cool breeze swept through the yard, Claire sat beside Scout, her hand resting gently on his fur. Scout looked up at her with those familiar eyes—soft, loyal, and full of love. It was as though he understood everything that had been said. The thought of losing him was unbearable, but Claire knew she had to let him go, just as Scout had always let her and the kids into his world. But not yet. Not today.

"We'll take you on one last chase, boy," Claire whispered softly, her voice catching in her throat. Scout's ears perked up, and though he didn't have the energy he once did, there was a spark in his eyes—a flicker of excitement.

The family gathered together the next weekend, a quiet understanding passing between them. The car was packed with water bottles, treats, and a leash for Scout, and they headed toward their favorite trail, the one that wove through the forest and stretched out toward the open fields. It was the place where Scout had run the hardest, the place where he had first raced with Ben and Lucy when they were little, where the laughter and the joy of being together had been as free as the wind.

When they reached the trailhead, Claire paused and knelt beside Scout. His movements were slower now, his tail wagging just a little as he sniffed at the familiar scents. He had been here so many times, but today felt different. His breathing was heavier, but still, he seemed to take in the world around him, his eyes bright with the memory of those earlier days.

"Ready, old boy?" James said, his voice thick with emotion as he rubbed Scout's ears. Ben and Lucy stood nearby, their faces a mix of excitement and sadness, watching their beloved dog prepare for what they all knew would be his last run.

With a gentle tug on his leash, Claire gave Scout a soft command, "Go, Scout. Go!"

And for the first time in months, Scout ran. His legs weren't as fast, his steps not as light as they had once been, but there was a joy in his movements that none of them had seen in a long time. Scout moved forward, his head held high, his body still remembering the feeling of the chase. The family followed at a slow pace, watching him with tears in their eyes, but their hearts full of love for the dog who had shared so much of his life with them.

They reached the open fields where the grass swayed in the wind, and Scout slowed to a stop, panting, his tail wagging gently. The family gathered around him, and they stood there in silence, taking in the moment, the memories, and the deep love that Scout had given them over the years.

Scout lay down in the tall grass, his body tired but content, his eyes closing as he rested in the warmth of the afternoon sun. He had given everything he had, and now, as his family sat beside him, he was at peace. There was no more running to be done, no more races to be won. His journey was coming to an end, but it had been a good one—a life full of love, joy, and adventure.

The family sat with him for a long time, not speaking, just being together in the quiet stillness. When the sun finally dipped below the horizon, Claire stood and gently patted Scout's head.

"We're so proud of you, boy," she said softly. "Thank you for all the love."

And with that, they walked back to the car, taking their time, savoring the final moments with the dog who had filled their lives with happiness.

But as they drove back to their home, something shifted in the air. Scout, resting in the backseat, let out a soft sigh, his body relaxing into the journey that would take him back to where it all began, to a place of rest. And though his time with them was ending, the family knew that Scout's love would continue to be a part of them, just as the wind carried his memory through the fields they had run together.

In the weeks that followed, the house felt quieter, but Scout's legacy lingered in the familiar places—his bed by the door, his favorite toys, the memories they would always carry with them. They knew that the true beauty of Scout's life had been in his unwavering loyalty, in the joy he had given them, and in the love he had shared. His final run, his last chase, had been a testament to the life they had shared together, and though he was gone, he would never be forgotten.

And so, the family learned that life wasn't about how fast you ran or how far you went—it was about the love you gave and the way you made others feel. That, in the end, was the greatest journey of all.

Silent Paws

Shadow had always known his purpose. He had been trained to guide, to protect, and to serve. From the moment he was paired with Noah, a young man who had lost his sight in a car accident, Shadow's life became intertwined with his handler's. The bond between them had grown strong over the years—Shadow was Noah's eyes, his legs when the ground was uneven, and his sense of security in a world filled with uncertainty. Together, they navigated the bustling streets, the busy shops, and the quiet parks, always side by side.

Noah had been Shadow's constant companion, and Shadow had been his. There was a rhythm to their lives, a quiet understanding between them. When Noah reached for his cane, Shadow would position himself to help guide him. When they crossed the street, Shadow would stop and wait for Noah to give the signal to move forward. Their communication was seamless, their connection effortless. The world was a little bit easier with Shadow by Noah's side.

But then, everything changed.

One chilly morning in the fall, as they were walking to the park—a route they had walked countless times—Shadow felt a sharp pain shoot up his leg. He hesitated for a moment, but kept moving, thinking it was just a strain, something that would pass. But as the day went on, the pain worsened. By the time they had reached the park, Shadow was limping. Noah noticed it too, his voice laced with concern.

"Shadow, what's wrong, boy?" Noah asked, kneeling beside his dog, his hand gently rubbing his leg.

Shadow sat down, his body trembling slightly as the pain continued to throb. He didn't want to let Noah down, but he couldn't hide the discomfort anymore. When they returned home, Noah examined his leg more carefully. There was swelling. Shadow's injury was more than just a strain. It was serious.

The vet's diagnosis was devastating. Shadow had torn a ligament in his leg, and it would take months for him to recover. The thought of not being able to work, of not being able to guide Noah, was unimaginable. Shadow had never known anything else—his purpose had always been to help, to lead, and now he was sidelined, unable to do the one thing he had been trained for.

The first few days after the injury were filled with confusion and frustration. Shadow lay on his bed, his leg elevated and bandaged, while Noah moved around the house, unsure of how to manage without him. The house, once filled with their steady routines, now felt disjointed. Noah had always relied on Shadow to help him navigate the world, but now, he had to depend on others. The sadness in Noah's eyes mirrored the emptiness that Shadow felt in his chest. The bond between them had been built on action, on trust, and now it was as if that bond had been broken.

One afternoon, Noah brought in a replacement guide dog—a young Labrador named Max. Max was eager, energetic, and ready to work. Noah tried to introduce Max to Shadow gently, hoping to ease the transition, but Shadow couldn't shake the feeling that his place had been taken. Max seemed to fill the space Shadow had once occupied, following Noah around, guiding him as Shadow had done. Shadow watched from the corner, his heart heavy, his body still aching, but it wasn't just the injury that pained him. It was the fear of being forgotten, of losing the bond he had shared with Noah.

Max was kind, but Shadow didn't want to give up. He would still nudge Noah when he needed to, still offer small licks of comfort when Noah sat in silence, still rest his head on Noah's lap at night. But no matter how hard he tried, he couldn't help but feel that the world was moving on without him. Max was becoming Noah's new eyes, and Shadow was just a dog, lying in the corner, trying to find a new place in a world that had changed.

Days turned into weeks, and Shadow's injury slowly began to heal, but the emotional pain seemed to linger longer. He missed the rhythm of their walks, the quiet communication, the bond that had once been effortless. He wanted to help, but the fear of failure was overwhelming. What if he could never be the guide dog Noah needed again?

One evening, as the sun began to set, Noah sat in his favorite chair, Max resting at his feet. Shadow, as he had done for years, walked over to Noah's side and sat down beside him. He looked up at Noah with soft eyes, unsure of what would come next.

Noah reached down and gently ran his fingers through Shadow's fur. For a long moment, there was silence between them—just the sound of the wind rustling outside, the soft creak of the floorboards beneath them. Then, Noah spoke quietly, his voice barely above a whisper.

"I'll never forget you, buddy. You've been my eyes for so long... You're still my best friend."

Tears welled up in Noah's eyes as he spoke, and Shadow nuzzled his hand gently, feeling the familiar warmth of their bond, a bond that couldn't be replaced. It was then that Shadow realized something. He didn't have to be Noah's guide anymore to be important. The love they shared wasn't just in the work they had done together. It was in every quiet moment, in every soft touch, in every shared silence.

Noah stood up slowly, taking a deep breath as he made his way to the door with Max at his side. He reached for Shadow's collar, gently guiding him toward the door as well. Shadow's heart fluttered with hope, but there was still uncertainty in his mind. Was this another way of saying goodbye?

But when they reached the park, Noah didn't ask Max to guide him. Instead, he let Shadow lead the way.

As they walked through the familiar paths, Shadow's pace was slower than before, his body still a little stiff, but there was something in his movements—something that reminded him of who he used to be. He didn't have to run anymore, didn't need to rush. He was still with Noah, still by his side, and that was enough.

Noah's voice was steady, filled with understanding as he spoke softly to Shadow.

"We're in this together, old boy. You'll always be my guide. Not just in the streets, but in life. You showed me how to see the world, even when I couldn't. And that's never going to change."

And with that, Shadow understood. He wasn't just a guide dog. He was Noah's companion, his friend, his partner. The work might have changed, but their bond had always been more than just function—it was love, deep and unwavering. Shadow realized then that even without the ability to guide, he still had a purpose. He would always have a place with Noah, no matter what.

Stars Above

Nova had always been a dog of the night. From the moment she was brought home as a puppy, she felt an unexplainable connection to the evening sky. Her owner, Sam, was an astronomer—his life was dedicated to the stars, the planets, and the vast mysteries of the universe. It was no surprise that Nova quickly became a constant companion in his nightly stargazing sessions.

Every evening, as dusk fell and the air grew cooler, Sam would carry Nova's favorite blanket to the backyard, setting up his telescope and lying back on the grass to look at the stars. Nova would curl up beside him, her eyes squinting up at the sky, sensing the quiet majesty of it all. She didn't understand the science behind the constellations or the galaxies, but she loved the peace it brought Sam. She could feel the calm in his breathing as they both took in the expanse above them.

"You see, Nova," Sam would say softly, his voice filled with wonder, "there's an entire universe up there, bigger than we can imagine. But it's all connected, just like us. Every star, every planet, part of something larger." Nova would nuzzle his side, her tail wagging as if she understood.

Sam had always been gentle with Nova, understanding her needs and her quiet ways. Their lives were filled with routine, with stargazing and quiet nights, their bond growing with each passing year. As Sam's career flourished, Nova remained his steadfast companion, always by his side as he spent hours working in his observatory or sharing a quiet moment under the stars. To Nova, the night sky had always been a place of comfort, a place where she could be with Sam, where everything felt as it should.

But as the years went by, Sam began to change. He grew quieter, more tired, and sometimes, he would sit alone in the dark, staring out at the stars with a distant look in his eyes. Nova, ever observant, noticed the shift. She stayed close, her body nestled against his, trying to comfort him as best as she could.

One winter evening, when the first snow had begun to fall softly around them, Sam sat in his usual spot in the backyard, gazing at the stars. Nova lay beside him, her head resting on his lap. But tonight, something felt different. Sam was still, too still, as the night stretched on. He hadn't said anything for a while, his hand absently stroking Nova's fur. The cold of the evening seemed to settle deeper into their bones, and Nova could sense a quiet sadness in the air that she couldn't understand.

The following weeks were harder. Sam's energy faded more quickly, and the trips to the hospital became more frequent. His love for the stars remained, but his body, worn from years of illness, no longer had the strength to keep up. Nova stayed by his side every step of the way, never leaving, never faltering in her loyalty. She could sense Sam's fading spirit, but all she could offer was her presence.

One morning, Sam's family told Nova that he was gone. They explained it gently, but Nova didn't understand. Sam had always been there for her, his voice filled with love and wonder as they looked at the stars together. But now, that voice was silent. The familiar scent of his presence was no longer around. Nova wandered through the house, looking for him, hoping to find him just around the corner, in the garden, or by the telescope in the observatory. But he was gone.

The house felt colder without him. The quiet was overwhelming. There were no more nights spent under the stars, no more conversations about the constellations or the wonders of the universe. There was only emptiness, and Nova felt it deeply.

But then, one evening, as the full moon rose high in the sky, Nova found herself standing alone in the backyard once again. The air was crisp, the snow glimmering beneath the light of the moon. She looked up at the stars, her breath misting in the cold night. For a moment, she simply stood there, listening to the stillness, her heart aching. The stars, which had always been a place of comfort, now seemed so far away.

As Nova stared up, something unexpected happened. It was as if the stars themselves were calling to her. The familiar constellations were just as bright, just as beautiful as they had always been, and she felt a soft warmth deep inside her. She could almost hear Sam's voice, gentle and steady, as if he were sitting beside her once again.

"Look, Nova," Sam had always said. "We're all part of this vast, interconnected universe. You and me, we're a part of it, too. Forever."

Tears welled in Nova's eyes as she stood there, the cool breeze brushing against her fur. She didn't know how long she had been standing there, but she suddenly understood. Sam had always told her that they were connected to something larger than themselves, and in that moment, she could feel it. She wasn't alone, not truly. Sam's love, his presence, was still with her, in the stars above and in her heart. Their bond had never been just about the earthly moments they had shared—it was eternal, as vast as the universe itself.

Nova sat down in the snow, her head turned toward the sky. For the first time since Sam's passing, she felt at peace. The stars weren't just distant lights; they were part of a cycle that would continue long after they were gone. Sam was a part of that cycle. And so, in her heart, was Nova.

As the moonlight bathed the garden in silver, Nova closed her eyes, letting the quiet night surround her. She had found her peace. Her journey, like the stars, was still unfolding, still part of a larger, infinite connection that she could not fully understand, but she could feel. And that, she knew, was enough.

Get Another Book Free

We love writing and have produced many books.

As a thank you for being one of our amazing readers, we'd like to offer you a free book.

To claim this limited-time offer, visit the site below and enter your name and email address.

You'll receive one of our great books directly to your email, completely free!

https://free.copypeople.com

---

1. https://free.copypeople.com

Did you love *Forever Friends: Heartbreaking and Touching Dog Stories*? Then you should read *Unicorn Magic Discovering the Wonders of a Hidden World*[2] by Morgan B. Blake!

Unicorn Magic: Discovering the Wonders of a Hidden World takes readers on a breathtaking journey into a realm where myths come alive and magic is more real than ever. With a collection of spellbinding tales, this book invites you into a world where unicorns—beings of beauty, mystery, and extraordinary power—return to confront ancient darkness, form unexpected bonds, and reveal the hidden magic woven into the fabric of the universe. From the reawakening of long-lost creatures to the secrets hidden within dreams, each story will take you to places where the impossible becomes reality.

---

2. https://books2read.com/u/mBR5JN

3. https://books2read.com/u/mBR5JN

In this mesmerizing collection, you'll meet dreamweavers who summon unicorns with their visions, a lonely gardener who hides a magical creature in his flowers, and a unicorn with a heart that contains the rarest of magics. Journey through enchanted gardens, hidden forests, and forgotten lands as you witness the struggles and triumphs of these mystical creatures. With lessons of balance, love, sacrifice, and the importance of dreams, *Unicorn Magic* offers not only a world of wonder but a poignant reflection on the power of imagination, inner strength, and connection.

Perfect for lovers of fantasy, magic, and adventure, *Unicorn Magic* reminds us all that the world is full of unseen wonders, just waiting to be discovered.

Also by Morgan B. Blake

The Hidden Truth
Silent Obsession

Standalone
Temporal Havoc
The AI Resurrection
99942 Apophis
The Shadows We Keep
Whispers of the Forgotten
Christmas Chronicles: Enchanted Stories for the Holiday Season
Realm of Enchantment Tales from the Mystic Lands
The Taniwha's Secret
Unicorn Magic Discovering the Wonders of a Hidden World
Vampire's Vow: Stories of Blood and Betrayal
Legends of the Damned: Villains Who Defied Fate and Conquered
All
Twisted Affection: How Love Can Break You
Lethal Beauty Inside the Minds of Women Who Kill
No One Left Behind Escaping the Shadow of War
The Spirit of Christmas: Heartwarming Stories of Holiday Magic
Forever Friends: Heartbreaking and Touching Dog Stories